D1741161

THE HUNGER

Fatefully Yours 7

Gabrielle Evans

**LOVEXTREME FOREVER
MANLOVE**

Siren Publishing, Inc.
www.SirenPublishing.com

A SIREN PUBLISHING BOOK
IMPRINT: LoveXtreme Forever ManLove

THE HUNGER
Copyright © 2011 by Gabrielle Evans

ISBN-10: 1-61926-107-3
ISBN-13: 978-1-61926-107-5

First Printing: October 2011

Cover design by Jinger Heaston
All art and logo copyright © 2011 by Siren Publishing, Inc.

ALL RIGHTS RESERVED: This literary work may not be reproduced or transmitted in any form or by any means, including electronic or photographic reproduction, in whole or in part, without express written permission.

All characters and events in this book are fictitious. Any resemblance to actual persons living or dead is strictly coincidental.

Printed in the U.S.A.

PUBLISHER
Siren Publishing, Inc.
www.SirenPublishing.com

THE HUNGER

Fatefully Yours 7

GABRIELLE EVANS
Copyright © 2011

Chapter One

Hex and Eyce stood side by side, a steel spreader holding their legs apart. Their wrists were bound together, their arms stretched over their heads where the ropes were connected to hooks in the ceiling.

Vapre was stretched out on his back in the center of the mattress, ankles and wrists bound to the bedposts with silk scarves. Syx knelt on the floor at the foot of the bed, his wrists tied behind him and a ball gag in his mouth.

Myst knelt in front of a wooden chair, his chest pressed flat to the seat and his wrists secured through the slats in the back. He wiggled his hips, showing off the bright blue butt plug lodged in his ass.

Echo almost swallowed his tongue as Fiero strutted toward him with a wicked glint in his eyes. "We"—he nodded to include Onyx—"know that you still have hang ups about being restrained. We just wanted to show you that it's not scary, and it can be a lot of fun. You'll be in complete control of everything that happens. Everyone is completely at your mercy."

"What about you two?" Echo asked. He didn't want to admit it yet, but the sight of his mates spread out before him like an all-you-can-eat buffet was having a very positive effect on his cock.

"If you want," Onyx answered immediately. "We really just want to watch."

"It turns you on?" Echo knew he loved to watch, but he didn't know Onyx and Fiero had the same kink.

Onyx groaned and rubbed at the sizeable lump behind his zipper. "Yeah, it does."

"So, what do you think?" Fiero asked. He wiggled his eyebrows playfully.

Echo smiled impishly. He'd be a moron to turn down such an opportunity. Each of his big, strong alpha mates was bound, hard, wanting, and turning to Echo for their pleasure. "I think I could learn to love surprises."

"I was hoping you'd say that." Onyx kissed his temple. "If anything gets to be too much, you just say the word and everything stops, okay?"

Echo nodded, but a confused frown tugged at the corners of his mouth. He wasn't the one being tied up. He would be doing all the playing. Why would any of it be too much for him?

Shrugging off the comment, Echo decided he wanted to tease his lovers a bit before they got down to the good stuff. "Strip and find a comfortable viewing position," he ordered Onyx and Fiero. He almost laughed when the warriors undressed eagerly and hurried over to the wall near the closet where two cushy armchairs sat side by side.

Onyx's comment still bothered him, but he tried to push it away. He'd been doing much better with Fiero's help over the past few weeks. He hardly ever freaked out when the demons restrained him anymore. Even when he did have a small twinge of unease, he'd found it wasn't hard to hide it until the pleasure overrode any fear or uncertainty.

Seeing his men bound and virtually helpless, turning over complete control to him, was a major turn-on. He was beginning to see why they liked doing it to him so much.

Moving slowly around the room, Echo undressed as he went, making a show of tugging his shirt over his head and popping open the button on his jeans. He put a little sway in his hips, closed his eyes, and moved sensuously to the imaginary beat inside his head.

He'd never really done anything like this before, and he hoped he was doing it right. If the quiet groans that reached his ears were any indication, he was. He eased his zipper down, still swaying his body from side and side and turning in slow circles so everyone in the room could see exactly what he was doing. He parted the fabric, pushed his jeans down his hips just enough for his leaking cock to bounce free, and gripped the turgid flesh in his palm.

The groans grew in volume, accompanied by a few rumbling growls and soft panting. Wiggling his hips, he let his jeans slide down his thighs and pool on the floor around his ankles. He stepped out of them easily, opening his eyes and grinning devilishly at the heated stares his mates were giving him.

With his fingers still wrapped around his straining cock, Echo stroked himself slowly, moaning in pleasure. He knew how much his men loved it when he moaned. After a few seconds, he released his heated length and knelt in front of Syx, shaking his head.

"Oh, this just won't do." Reaching behind the warrior, he unbuckled the soft leather holding the rubber ball in Syx's mouth and eased it away gently before dropping it to the floor. "I want to hear you," he whispered seductively.

Syx's gaze traveled over Echo's body, his eyes flashing with heat and passion as he licked his swollen lips. "Whatever you want, sweetheart."

"Oh, I like the way that sounds." Echo pushed up and flicked his tongue over Syx's lips. "I'll be back." Then he rose gracefully to his feet and sauntered across the carpeted floor to stand in front of Hex and Eyce.

Eyce shuddered when Echo ran his fingertips lightly over the warrior's chest. "Mmm, so big and strong," Echo purred. His hand wrapped around Eyce's jutting cock, stroking him slowly as he bent at the waist to lap at the clear drops of pre-cum that beaded on the tip. His lover growled and tensed, and his hips jerked forward as much as his position would allow.

Smirking, Echo released him and stood straight. He walked around Eyce once before moving on to Hex. "Beautiful," he whispered reverently, running both hands down Hex's sculpted back, over his lean hips, and finally cupping his mate's ass and squeezing the muscled globes. Hex shivered but didn't make a sound. "I'm going to make you scream for me, Hex."

Still, their alpha said nothing.

Echo skimmed his nose down Hex's spine, breathing in the clean scent from the demon's recent shower. Oh, Hex smelled good enough to eat.

Lowering to his knees, Echo whispered his fingertip down Hex's crease, smiling to himself when the cheeks clenched and relaxed against his touch. Spreading his lover open, Echo eyed the pretty, pink starburst, watching as it fluttered and twitched, practically begging for his touch.

Leaning closer, he breathed warm air over his lover's hole then pushed his tongue out to swirl and lick around the guarding muscles. He licked and laved, his fingers digging into Hex's ass cheeks. When he still received no verbal response from his lover, Echo pointed his tongue and thrust inside Hex's hole.

Hex trembled and a quiet groan, not much more than a shaky breath, escaped his parted lips. Smiling in satisfaction, Echo rocked back on his heels and rose to his feet. "Was that so hard?"

He didn't expect a reply, so he didn't wait for one. Taking slow, deliberate steps, he prowled toward the bed, his eyes raking over Vapre's nude body, drinking in the sight of all the gorgeous pale skin.

Vapre watched him approach with heavy-lidded eyes. His tongue darted out to moisten his lips, and the muscles in his arms bunched as he strained against the bindings on his wrist. His long, veiny cock flexed, rising up from his belly as though waving hello to Echo.

Easing down on the side of the bed, Echo let his waist-length hair slip down the front of one shoulder as he leaned over his mate. He crawled up Vapre's body then wiggled back down, letting the silky strands ghost over Vapre's chest, abs, and groin. The warrior shivered, his hips arching up from the mattress so that his weeping cock rubbed against Echo's. "You are killing me here, babe."

Echo chuckled softly, placed a quick kiss on Vapre's hip and rolled off the bed. "Patience," he scolded lightly.

Two long strides, and Echo dropped to his knees, molding himself to Myst's back. Insinuating a hand between their heated bodies, he tapped at the base of the butt plug. "So sexy," he whispered into the damp skin between his lover's shoulder blades.

He gripped the flat base, wiggled it a little. He pulled it out partially then let Myst's tight channel suck it right back in. Myst groaned, dropping his forehead to the seat of the chair between his elbows. "Please."

"Please what?" Echo felt like a freaking god. His men all desired him, yet relied solely on him for their pleasure. They couldn't even touch themselves. He could quickly become addicted to this.

"More," Myst whispered.

"In a minute." Echo kissed the side of Myst's neck and crawled across the floor to where Fiero and Onyx sat watching the show. "Uh-uh," he chided them.

The warriors looked at each other, then to Echo, and released the hold on their swollen cocks with identical sighs of disappointment. "Ah, c'mon, Echo," Fiero half whined. It was actually kind of cute.

Echo responded by diving forward and capturing the bright red tip of Fiero's cock between his lips. He twirled his tongue around the engorged crown, slid his lips down the hot length, then dragged them back up as he hollowed his cheeks and sucked hard.

The warrior hissed in a breath through his teeth, lifting up from the chair and forcing his dick further into Echo's mouth. Quiet groans went through the room, and Echo smiled around the hard flesh in his mouth.

He worked his lover's glistening cock for a minute longer then popped off with a naughty slurp. Licking his numb, swollen lips, Echo turned his attention to Onyx, engulfing the warrior's prick to the back of his throat in one swift movement. While he was enjoying himself immensely, his own dick throbbed and jerked, his balls ached, and his sphincter clenched greedily.

They needed to get this show on the road, so to speak.

Pulling off of Onyx, Echo rose to his feet and turned his head slowly, working out the logistics in his head. He wanted to watch this time, just watch while his men loved one another in various ways. Sometimes he needed to feel them all together, to know they were connected. This wasn't one of those times.

"Fiero, suck Eyce's cock."

Both demons groaned, and Eyce's eyes actually rolled back in his head. Fiero jumped up without a word and hurried across the room to Eyce. He planted a searing kiss on their lover's lips before sliding down his body and swallowing Eyce's dick until his nose pressed against the demon's groin.

"Onyx, fuck Myst." It was a damn good thing his men liked it when he was bossy, because he couldn't hold back. He had an image in his head of how it all should work, and he wanted to see it come to life. It was as though they were his own personal Ken dolls to do with as he pleased, and he intended to take full advantage.

Onyx rose from his chair immediately and stroked his heavy erection as he stalked toward Myst. He didn't waste time with kisses and cuddles—just eased the toy from Myst's hole, lined up the bulbous head of his cock, and pushed into Myst's slicked entrance hard and fast.

Echo trembled and moaned, stroking his own dick as he watched Onyx wrap an arm around Myst's waist and began pounding into him like a man possessed. "Slow, Onyx. Fuck him slow, so I can enjoy watching you two together."

The warrior's thrust slowed until he moved almost lazily, his thick cock disappearing into Myst's body over and over in long, languid strokes.

"Gonna," Eyce grunted from the other side of the room.

Echo swung around, jerking his throbbing dick and watching Eyce tense and Fiero swallow quickly. "Get him down," he breathed.

Fiero licked Eyce clean then stood and lifted the rope from the hook in the ceiling, letting Eyce's arms fall to rest in front of him. "What now?" he asked Echo. "This is your show, baby. Whatever you want. Just tell us, and we'll do it."

His eyes flickered to Hex, and Echo smiled lecherously. "Make him come."

Two minutes later, Fiero had the spreader removed from Eyce's ankles, but didn't remove the binds from his wrist. Eyce moved fluidly, dropping to his knees and encircling Hex's prick with his lips. Fiero stood behind Hex, running his hands up the demon's chest and pinching at his nipples. "Gonna fuck you until you scream," he rumbled to Hex, but loud enough that everyone could hear.

Echo's sac tightened, his heart hammered, sweat beaded across his skin, and he struggled to drag in air to his lungs. When his lower belly cramped and his dick swelled in his hand, he released the hard flesh, snatched the lube up from the foot of the bed, and moved behind Syx.

"Gotta get you ready, love." He helped Syx move toward the bed, then pressed between his massive shoulder blades until his mate's chest rested flat against the mattress. Slicking his fingers, he slid the trembling digits between Syx's parted cheeks and rubbed circles over the fluttering starburst.

"Just hurry," Syx panted, rolling his forehead against the comforter on the bed.

Taking him at his word, Echo pushed inside Syx's silky channel with two fingers, working them in and out quickly until he could add a third. Looking up the bed, Echo smiled at Vapre, his balls tingling at the heated look in the man's eyes.

When he had Syx's hole slicked and loosened, he urged the warrior to his feet and nodded in Vapre's direction. "Ride him, Syx."

His mate licked his lips and nodded, the sinews of his arms flexing as he pulled against the restraints. Echo touched his lover's hands where they were bound together just over Syx's lower back and shook his head. "Just like this. Please."

"Whatever you want," Syx whispered and bent to crush his mouth to Echo's in a toe-curling kiss. They worked together to get Syx on the bed and straddling Vapre's hips. Echo took Vapre's weeping cock in hand, stroked the demon a few times, then held him at attention while Syx hovered over the swollen crown.

So slowly, Echo just knew Syx was trying to torture him, the warrior lowered himself over Vapre's cock, impaling himself until his firm ass nestled against Vapre's groin. They all three moaned and shuddered, and Echo grabbed the base of his dick to keep from blowing his load right then and there.

"What about you?" Vapre asked seductively when Syx began to rise and lower over him.

"I want to watch." With that said, Echo rolled off the mattress and backed away, his eyes never leaving the erotic show on the bed. Easing into Fiero's recently vacated chair, Echo planted his heels on the seat beside his ass and spread his legs wide.

His hand moved over his pulsing length in a blur, and he pushed two still-oiled fingers into his needy hole. His eyes traveled to Hex, eating up the smooth, glistening skin, the rolling of his muscles, and the mingled look of pleasure, pain, and love on his ridiculously handsome face.

Though the biggest and toughest of them all, Hex surrendered beautifully to Fiero and Eyce. There was no pride, no fear, no indication that he didn't trust them fully with every part of his body.

Fiero's arms kept a tight hold on Hex's hips, his fingers digging into the supple flesh as he pounded into Hex's upturned ass in lightning fast strokes. Every punishing thrust sent Hex's hips jerking forward, pushing his cock deeper and deeper into Eyce's willing mouth.

Inserting a third finger into his clenching opening, Echo pumped his fingers, his other hand jerking furiously at his cock as it swelled almost painfully in his tight grip.

His eyes wandered to Onyx next, drinking in the delicious sight of the demon's long length plunging into Myst's hot hole. Again, Onyx held the power, but Myst looked more than happy to give it to him. The warrior's fingers curled around the slats in the back of the chair, and he rocked with Onyx, pushing back against him and groaning loudly.

Finally turning his attention to Syx and Vapre, Echo's body tensed, while electricity raced down his spine to pool and burn in his aching balls. Syx's head fell back on his shoulders, his wrists still tied behind his back, and he lifted up on his knees before dropping back down quickly. Vapre moved as much as he could with his ankles secured to the bedposts, arching his back, and pushing his cock further into Syx's ass.

Echo's orgasm slammed into him, taking him by surprise and robbing the breath from his lungs. "Fuck!" He cried out loudly, his hips snapped upward, and hot cream erupted from the end of his cock to land on his belly, chest, and even his neck.

Several loud moans and growls followed his completion. The sounds of damp skin slapping together increased in volume and tempo, keeping the steady beat to the music of the warriors' own cries of release.

It had been one of the most intense orgasms Echo had ever had, yet he'd received no other touch than his own. He finally began to understand what Fiero and Onyx were trying to tell him—show him. It wasn't so much about control or power play. It was the faith that your partner would take care of you, catch you if you fell, and never neglect that trust.

His warriors always gave him what he needed, taking only a little for themselves, and never showed him any reason to doubt them. Though they all liked his bossy side, maybe it was time to show a little more submissiveness.

"Someone order pizza. I'm starving and need a shower." Echo pushed up from his chair, winked, and blew air kisses to his men.

Yeah, he'd get right on that passiveness…later.

Chapter Two

Onyx kissed the side of Myst's neck and eased out of his clutching hole. "Thank you," he whispered.

"Always my pleasure," Myst responded breathlessly.

Untying his lover, Onyx massaged the man's wrists and arms, working the circulation back into them. "You okay, baby?"

Myst stiffened a bit at the endearment, and Onyx bit his lip, waiting for Myst's reaction. Then the warrior relaxed, pushing up straight and brushing their lips together. "I'm great." His mouth stretched into a wide grin against Onyx's. "Better than great." He trailed kisses along Onyx's jawline and rubbed their cheeks together. "You can call me baby whenever you want," he said very quietly.

Palming the back of Myst's head, Onyx held him for just a moment, kissed his temple, then rose to his feet. He watched while Fiero and Eyce disconnected Hex from the hook over his head, and Myst moved to help unbind Vapre and Syx. With everyone preoccupied, he slipped into the bathroom and made his way directly to the shower.

Stepping inside the steamy shower stall, his breath caught in his throat at the beautiful sight Echo made as the heated water fell over his tight little body. "Are you okay?"

Echo turned slowly, lifted his arms and waited for Onyx to walk into them. His slim fingers wrapped around the back of Onyx's neck, and Echo pulled him down into a sweet kiss. "I'm starting to get it. Just be patient with me."

"Oh, baby, it's not like that. Me and Fiero, we like to play rough sometimes, but we don't have to do that with you if it makes you uncomfortable. You're doing so much better, and I haven't seen you freak once in weeks. If it still makes you nervous, you don't have to do it. Just tell us, and everything stops, okay?"

Echo giggled, a rare sound for him, and placed his hand over Onyx's mouth to cut off his rambling. "It is getting easier. I know Fiero likes to tie me up. I don't exactly get why, but if that's his kink, why should he have to change for me? The things that happened to me before are not the same. I just have to remember that, and I'll be fine."

He moved his hand when Onyx nodded. "You." Echo smirked and shook his head. "You are always so careful with me. You've only lost control once, and then avoided me for days afterward. I know you like to play rough. I'm not sure what all that entails, but I want to try for you."

Onyx closed his eyes and breathed deeply. Echo had no idea what he was saying. Sure, he'd held up to the restraints that Fiero liked to play with. He'd done well with the spankings. Onyx wanted more, and he honestly didn't think his tiny little mate would be so understanding toward his particular kink.

"I want to try," Echo repeated. "We can stop if I don't like it, right?"

Onyx opened his eyes, staring straight into Echo's, and nodded hesitantly. Yes, he would stop at any time if Echo gave the word. If it came to that, however, he feared it would damage something between them that couldn't be fixed. Not because he would be angry or disappointed, but because he didn't think he could stand to see the distrust and fear in Echo's eyes.

"I'd never hurt you," he finally said. No, he wouldn't, but then Echo was just so small, and his idea of pleasurable pain was probably very different than Onyx's.

"I know you won't." Echo grabbed a washcloth, soaped it thoroughly, and began washing Onyx's chest and arms. "I'm not as fragile as you think I am, love. Let me be the judge of what I can and can't handle."

"I just don't want you to be afraid of me. Ever." Closing his eyes, he tried to enjoy the feel of his mate's hands on him, but the worry niggled in the back of his head.

"As long as you stop if I ask, I won't be afraid." Warm lips wrapped around Onyx's pebbled nipple, and he moaned softly, pushing closer to Echo's mouth. "We'll talk about it later. Right now, just stop thinking and let me take care of you."

Onyx didn't want to think anymore anyway. Thinking hurt his head and just left him more confused than when he started. Spreading his legs further apart, he lifted his arms to his sides and just basked in Echo's loving attention. His muscles relaxed, his breathing became slow and heavy, and his insides felt warm and gooey.

"Why can't I go into town alone?" Echo whispered.

With his brain swimming on a blissful high, Onyx answered without thought. "Because someone would try to take you from us."

"What about the people at the party?"

"They're different."

"What makes them different?"

"They're different," Onyx repeated, moaning when Echo's fingers began to massage his heavy ball sac. Some resemblance of reason returned to him, and he refused to trek further into the conversation. Hex said he would explain it to Echo later. He must have a reason, and Onyx would respect that. "Don't try to trick me."

"Okay, I'll let it go for now, but I think I have the right to know."

"Talk to Hex." Onyx dropped his head forward, his chin resting against his chest, and focused on the feel of Echo's dainty hands against his slippery skin. Gods, his mate's hands were so soft.

"Oh, I intend to talk to him. I guess he needs a little reminder of what happens when he keeps things from me."

Onyx chuckled under his breath as he remembered the last reminder. He'd thought Hex as going to piss himself when Echo threw that fireball in his direction. Echo was feisty as hell, and Onyx wouldn't have it any other way. Lifting his head just enough to look into Echo's eyes, he smiled warmly. "Love you, yeah?"

Echo mirrored his smile, rising up on his tiptoes to press their lips together. "Love you, too, my crazy warrior. Always."

Before he could wipe the sappy grip from his mouth and form a coherent response, the glass door slid open, Eyce and Fiero stepping into the shower behind Onyx.

"Yum," Echo breathed, licking his lips and arching his eyebrow. He waved a hand toward Onyx's groin, then to the other demons, indicating the jutting cocks standing out from between their legs. "For me?"

"We didn't even get to touch you," Eyce pouted.

Onyx didn't bother to hide his laughter. "Poor baby," he teased.

"Well, I think I can solve that for you," Echo purred as he stepped past Onyx, making sure to slide against him as he went. He rubbed against Fiero first then showed the same attention on Eyce until both men were panting.

A wicked smiled ghosted over Echo's face, his hand reaching behind him to slide open the shower door. "Now you've touched me." He stepped backward out of the shower and slid the door shut in their shocked faces.

"What the hell just happened?" Fiero growled in frustration.

Onyx laughed again, though his cock was hard enough to pound railroad spikes. "I think he's playing hard to get."

"You do know I can still hear you, right?" Echo called from the other side of the glass. "I'm not playing hard to get. I'm simply holding out so that you'll appreciate it more when you get it."

"What the fuck is the difference?" Fiero demanded.

The door opened once more. Echo smiled impishly at them, and Onyx had a feeling he wasn't going to like the answer. "There's not one. My way just makes me sound like less of a slut. Besides"—Echo turned and walked across the room—"you know how much you love to chase me."

He disappeared into the bedroom, and Onyx looked up at his lovers. "What now?"

Eyce flew out of the shower, wrenched open the door, and hurried out of the bathroom. Fiero growled, almost falling on his face in his haste to follow Eyce. Onyx shut off the shower and chuckled under his breath.

"And the chase is on."

* * * *

"Why don't you erase some of these?" Myst gestured toward Syx's dry erase board that hung on the office wall. "I mean, we know where the money went that was stolen. You could mark that one off the list of shit we don't know."

Syx shook his head. "We assume that Ares conned Lexi into transferring the money. We have no proof. Until I have factual evidence, it stays."

"Echo says he was in that compound all of his life. If Ares is really involved with that lab, if he's heading the operations, do you honestly believe that he's been planning this for the last twenty-three years?"

"Time is different in the realm of immortals," Syx replied simply as though that explained everything.

Myst wasn't buying it. "Yeah, I guess, but I still think we're missing something. I mean, if he's so bent on having Echo, why not take him while he was in the lab and under his thumb?" He shoved a hand through his dark, shaggy locks and tugged. "And why try to kill him? It doesn't make sense, Syx."

"I've been wondering that myself. Every time he shows up, he makes a big deal about wanting Echo. Then he not only tries to kill him, but succeeds."

Myst's chest tightened, and he rubbed at it with the heel of his palm. If he lived forever—which was a very real possibility—he'd never be able to repay the goddess, Athena, for the gift she'd granted them by returning their mate. So what if he was a little different now and needed their blood to live? He was still their Echo, and Myst couldn't imagine his life without the man.

"Hey," Syx said quietly, stepping closer and cupping the side of Myst's face. "Echo is safe. In fact, I have a feeling that he's much more durable now than he was before."

"We should have protected him." What Myst really meant was that *he* should have protected Echo. They'd come so close to losing much more than some fucking war, all because they'd been too wrapped up in bickering amongst themselves to keep an eye on their little mate.

"Yes, we should have," Syx agreed. "It's over now, and there is nothing we can do about it. We've been given a second chance, and we both know how rare those are. Now, we make sure that Athena's gift was not given in vain."

"He goes nowhere without one of us." Myst's chest vibrated as he growled.

"Stop being all grumbly. Echo understands the danger now. He'll be more careful. We're not going to lose him, okay?"

Nodding reluctantly, Myst breathed in through his nose, trying to tamp down the rage building inside him. He was going to enjoy tearing Ares apart slowly.

Syx kissed his temple before stepping away to scribble something on the whiteboard. "So, we need to figure out what is really going on with Ares and what he's after. I'm with you in thinking that he's using Echo as a diversionary tactic."

"What about Hex?" Myst's fingers curled into his palm to form a tight fist. "He's had a semi for Hex for three thousand years."

"You think he'd go to war just to take Hex to his bed?" Syx lifted both eyebrows skeptically. "The man's sexy as sin, but that seems a little extreme, even for Ares."

"Well, whatever the reason, I think we stand a better chance of winning if we know what he's after."

"I agree completely. We have time to figure it out, though. We need to be focusing on the next test right now. There's only two left, and I can't imagine that they'll be easy."

Myst chewed on his lip and nodded. His stomach churned and cramped, threatening to send dinner racing back up his esophagus. His test was coming. He had no way of knowing what it would be, but his instincts screamed that it would be the hardest of them all. Something gnawed at his nerves, niggled at his brain, and sent his heart racing.

Whatever was to come, he'd face it. He had no choice. Going by the prophecy, he doubted he'd be worrying about dying crops. That had Onyx written all over it, which only left battling back enemies that were determined to destroy those "born of the first." He didn't have a damn clue what that meant or how to fight against it.

"We'll find a way," Syx said quietly. "You're not alone."

Myst nodded again but didn't answer. He knew the warrior was only trying to comfort him and lend his support. "I'm going to find Echo." He'd done a damn fine job of depressing himself, and he wanted his mate. Echo always made everything disappear, at least for a little while.

"I think he's upstairs badgering Hex to explain why he can't go into town alone." Syx rolled his eyes. "I don't know why Hex won't just spit it out. There's not a whole lot that Echo can't handle, and he's faced way worse than this."

"Do Jet and Pax know?"

Syx shook his head. "No, and we want to keep it that way for now. We've flown under the radar for the most part. Jet and Pax are going to be curious, and I honestly can't blame them. We need them right now, though, and we need to stick together."

After thinking it over for a minute, Myst tilted his head to the side and frowned. "Are you sure they don't know? I thought they could smell it."

Syx's eyes widened, and he smacked himself in the forehead with his palm. "Fuck!"

"We need to talk to them." Myst scratched at the back of his neck. "If we explain to them why we need them here for now, I think they'd understand."

"We have to tell them," Syx agreed grudgingly. "It's too dangerous for them to not have all the details. Why haven't they said anything, though?"

Myst shrugged. "You said we needed to talk to them. Let's go find out."

Syx chuckled and gave Myst a little shove toward the door. "You sound better."

"I like having something to do. Sitting around and waiting for bad shit to happen sucks. I just want all this crap to be over with."

"Me and you both, babe." Syx ruffled Myst's hair. "You and me both."

Chapter Three

Onyx stepped into the living room from the kitchen just as Syx and Myst entered from the hallway. "Hey, have you guys seen Jet or Pax?"

Myst and Syx shared a look that Onyx couldn't decipher, but it didn't look good. "Uh, when's the last time you saw them?" Myst asked. Onyx could tell he was trying for nonchalant, but he didn't quite pull it off.

"The night of the new moon. We came home, they went to their rooms, and I don't think I've seen them since. I thought they might be hiding out because they were ashamed of what happened. By the looks on your faces, I'd say that's not the case."

"We were just coming to find them," Syx admitted. He pulled at his blond hair and sighed. "This is bad."

"You think they left?" Onyx ground his teeth together to keep from growling. "How could they just slip out without any of us knowing about it?"

"It's not like we exactly keep tabs on them like we do Echo," Myst answered indignantly.

"Keep tabs on who?" Fiero strolled into the room, shoving a chocolate cupcake into his mouth. "Wha' goin' on?"

Without looking Fiero's way, Onyx reached out and smacked the warrior in the back of the head. "Don't talk with your mouth full."

Fiero opened his mouth and stuck his tongue out to show off the gooey glob in his mouth. Then he shut his lips and swallowed before smiling roguishly at Onyx. "Yes, Mother."

Onyx cuffed him in the back of the head again. "Have you seen the shifters?"

Shrugging, Fiero sauntered over to the sofa and plopped down on the cushions, sprawling out as though it was no concern to him. "Nope."

"What about the bloodsuckers and Craze?" Myst asked slowly. "Have they been around?"

"Haven't seen 'em in a couple of days," Fiero answered distractedly while he flipped through the channels on the television.

Onyx tensed. "Gage, Mac, or Sony?"

"Saw Mac this morning," Syx said immediately. "I haven't seen Gage or Sony, though. Mac looked like shit, and he didn't say too much."

"Son of a bitch," Onyx growled. "Split up and check the house. We'll meet back here in five minutes."

Five minutes later, everyone was back, Syx dragging Mac along behind him. Mac knew something, but he wasn't talking. He wouldn't meet Onyx's eyes either. "Call Craze."

Syx pulled his cell phone from his pocket and began dialing.

"I'll get Hex," Myst offered and turned to jog back up the stairs.

"I'll go find the others." Then Fiero disappeared as well.

"Straight to voice mail." Syx flipped his phone closed and stuffed it back in his pocket. "I really do not have the patience for this shit right now."

That was saying something considering Syx had to be the most patient and easygoing of them all. "Do you think they left on their own?"

"Well, I sure as hell don't think someone walked in here and took them without any of us knowing," Eyce said, following Fiero down the staircase. "I can't believe Craze wouldn't tell us, though. He knows how dangerous it is."

As one, they all turned their eyes to Mac. "You need to tell us what you know," Onyx said. "Why would you just let Gage go like that?"

"He didn't tell me he was leaving," Mac whispered, finally lifting his head to meet Onyx's gaze. "I woke up, and they were gone."

"Then why didn't you tell someone?" Syx asked gently.

"Gage left a note. He said for me to stay in our room, that he'd be back soon, and not to tell anyone."

"Did it say anything about where he was going?" Hex asked as he and Echo followed Myst into the room.

Mac shook his head. His eyes were red and puffy, glittering with unshed tears. "No. I'm sorry."

"When did they leave?"

"The night after the new moon. I woke up the next morning, and they were gone."

That had been the night Onyx and his lovers had gone down to the kappa pound to have a little time alone. It had been a nice night, warmer than usual. They'd fed cucumbers to the kappas, made love under the stars, and just enjoyed spending some uninterrupted time together.

"What about the others?" Syx asked. "They're all missing."

Mac shook his head again. "I don't know. Someone please tell me what's going on. Are they okay?"

"I don't think so, Mac." Onyx wished he had better news for the little man. If Gage had thought to be back before anyone noticed, and he'd yet to return, that could only mean things had not gone as planned.

"You haven't seen anything?" Fiero asked. He tapped his temple to punctuate how he thought Mac would have *seen*.

"I'm not a fucking transistor radio!" Mac shouted. His chest heaved, rising and falling in rapid succession. "I can't just tune into whatever channel I want to see. It doesn't work that way!"

Echo hurried over to his friend and wrapped an arm around Mac's shoulders. "We're going to find them, okay?" He looked at Hex and glared. "Now do you see what happens when you keep secrets?" he asked dangerously.

Onyx wasn't exactly happy with their leader either, but it wasn't the time to start arguing. "We need to talk to Lorcan."

Echo closed his eyes and groaned. "That had better not be another secret ex-lover, or I promise you, I'm about to become really freakin' celibate."

"No." Hex scrubbed a hand over his face and took a deep breath. "He's the alpha of the local pack."

"Pack of what?" If there had been any more ice in Echo's voice, the room would have frozen over solid.

"Coyote shifters," Onyx answered when Hex merely continued to stare. This had gone on long enough. "Lorcan is a good guy. You met him."

Echo's eyebrows drew together, and he mumbled under his breath for a few seconds. "That huge guy from the party that owns a flower shop in town?"

"Yep. That's him. If he knows anything, he'll help."

"He seemed really nice when I met him." Echo's brow creased further. "Why would you want me to stay away from him?"

"Oh, it's not the coyotes that we're worried about," Hex answered. "The pack doesn't live in town. They have a little community set up a little ways west."

"Hex," Echo growled. "Would you just spit it out already? I think I've proven that there is very little that I can't handle."

Onyx agreed. He was all for protecting their mate, and keeping him away from undue stress, but Echo had a right to know— especially after the things that had happened to him in the past few weeks. "Just tell him, Hex. I don't know why it's such a big goddamn secret anyway."

Hex nodded curtly before returning his attention to Echo. "Lorcan informed us a few days before the party that there were some newcomers to the town. He thinks they're running from something, and a couple members of his pack have gone missing. Not to mention regular townspeople."

"You mean humans," Echo deciphered. "Okay, so that leads me to believe that these drifters are *not* human." He rubbed at his temples and sighed. "Hex, please, I'm begging here. Can we cut through all the bullshit and just get to the point?"

"They're vampires, Echo."

Echo didn't say anything for a long time, and Onyx could tell their mate was turning over the information in his head. He could practically hear the wheels turning.

"That's why you immediately thought I had been changed when you found me," he said slowly. "I would imagine that Ares planned it that way as well. If I'd had died like I was supposed to, you would have ripped the town apart to find out who did it."

Onyx wasn't sure whether to growl at the idea of someone hurting his mate, or smile at Echo's perceptiveness. In the end, he settled for a little snarl. Hey, at least his lip curled upward.

"So, everyone that has been here is from Lorcan's pack, huh?"

The warriors all nodded.

"It would have been easier if you'd just told me." Echo huffed and shook his head. "Okay, we're going to talk about this later, and about how it's stupid to keep things from me. Right now, I want to know what's going on and why everyone is missing."

"We've been pulled in six different directions for the past few months," Onyx began. "When we invited the shifters to celebrate your birthday, we didn't even think about Jet and Pax. I'm sure they're pretty eager to learn more about the local pack after being isolated their entire lives."

"That makes sense, but why wouldn't they just tell us?" Echo looked kind of cute when he was confused. His nose scrunched and his lips were pouty. "I mean, we could have invited the pack here where it's safe. Why would they just leave like that?"

"I think they were ashamed of what they did on the new moon," Syx responded. "Maybe they thought they wouldn't be welcome here anymore."

"That's ridiculous." Echo threw his hands up and marched over to flop down on the sofa. "And it doesn't explain where everyone else went either. You're going to have to do better than that."

"Echo, we don't have all the answers. If we did, we wouldn't be standing around with our dicks in our hands right now."

Echo glared at Fiero and stuck his tongue out. "Well, someone call Lorcan and find out what he knows. Or go look for them. I don't know why Gage would take Sony and leave Mac here. That doesn't make a damn bit of sense."

Onyx shifted his eyes to Mac. The little guy looked so lost that it broke his heart. He'd probably have the same look if he suddenly found himself alone, and specifically, without his men. "Mac, have you tried to call him?"

Mac shook his head sadly. "I don't have a phone. I would have had to ask to borrow one of yours, and then you'd know Gage was gone. He told me not to tell anyone."

Hex's hand shot into his pocket, drawing Onyx's attention. The alpha pulled his cell phone out, stared at the display, and then flipped it open. "Lorcan, I was just about to call you."

He was silent for a long time, his face completely wiped of any emotion. "I see. I don't know if that's a good idea. You know why they're here." He paused again and finally sighed. "Right. Right. No, I get it." Another moment of silence. "Thank you, Lorcan. We'll take help wherever we can find it. We're missing a few other members of the house as well. Do you know anything about that?"

Onyx drifted closer to Hex without even realizing it. Whatever was going on, he wanted to know, and he wanted to know *now*.

"Okay. Right. I'll be in touch soon." Hex flipped his phone closed and shoved it in his pocket. "That was Lorcan."

Everyone growled, and Eyce actually smacked Hex in the back of the head. "No shit," Eyce grumbled. "What did he say?"

"Jet and Pax are with his pack. I guess they showed up last night."

"So, we're correct in assuming they were just curious?" Syx asked.

Hex shook his head. "They met Lorcan at the party."

Onyx bit the inside of his cheek until it bled to keep from snapping at Hex. His patience was running thin, and the demon's hedging was just pissing him off.

"Lorcan is their mate." Hex pinched the bridge of his nose and breathed deeply. "Lorcan told them to stay here until he could make it safe for them to join his pack."

"So, why did they leave?" Echo asked.

Onyx smiled at his mate and shook his head. "What would you do if we sent you away—even if it was for your own safety—and didn't tell you how long it would be before we came for you?"

"I'd hunt you down and kick your ass," Echo responded immediately.

"Exactly. It's worse for shifters, vampires, even demons." Eyce drifted over to the sofa and eased down beside Echo. "It's like this clawing, aching, all-consuming need to be near our mates. You can only fight it for so long."

"I still don't know why they didn't just tell us."

Everyone turned to look at Hex. "Well, Syx nailed in on the head about them being ashamed and not thinking they were welcome here any longer." Hex waved a hand as if the information was unimportant. "Anyway, they're going to stay with Lorcan for now. He's also offered the aid of his pack in the war."

"I knew I liked him," Echo quipped with a big smile. "I will miss Jet and Pax, though. They'll still visit, right?"

Onyx shrugged. Yeah, the little shifters were nice, but he wasn't too upset about them leaving. As long as they were safe, it was one step closer to having their home back to themselves. "Did he know anything about Gage or the rest of them?"

"He says he doesn't, and I believe him."

Onyx retrieved his phone from his pocket and shoved it into Mac's hands. "Call Gage."

"Rude," Echo called from the sofa.

"Please," Onyx bit out then turned a frosty grin on his mate. "Better, dear?"

"Not really."

Before anyone could say or do anything, the front door swung open, and Craze stomped into the living room. He looked mad enough to breathe fire, and he was completely alone. He held up a hand before any of them could question him, though. "I don't want to talk about it right now. Let me get a shower and calm down, and I'll tell you everything I know."

With that, he turned on his heels and marched up the staircase.

"This just keeps getting better." Echo sighed and curled into Eyce's side. "I quit."

"What do you quit?" Eyce asked quietly.

"Trying to figure out all the answers. I just want someone to tell me what to do from now on so I don't have to think anymore."

Onyx swallowed down the groan that he felt rumbling in his chest. Just maybe, he was exactly what their mate needed at the moment. He sure as hell hoped so, anyway. Walking slowly across the room, he stopped in front of Echo and held out his hand. "Come with me."

Echo looked confused but took his hand and rose gracefully from the sofa. "Where are we going?"

"Go up to my room and wait for me. I'll be there in a minute."

To his surprise, Echo didn't argue. He dipped his head once and disappeared from the room.

"Be careful with him," Fiero warned. "He's getting better, but I'm not sure if he's ready for you, man."

"I'd never hurt him," Onyx vowed.

"We know." Vapre's fingers wound around the back of Onyx's neck, and he squeezed gently. "All we're saying is that he's not one of us. Go slow."

"I'd never hurt him," Onyx repeated. "If things don't go…right…"

"We'll give you whatever you need," Myst answered Onyx's unspoken question. "Hell, I'll give it to you even if things go perfectly."

With that reassurance, Onyx took a deep breath and went in search of his mate. He'd never been nervous before, but then again, he'd never had so much riding on how he conducted himself or how his partner would perceive him. He just hoped he didn't fuck this up.

Chapter Four

Echo sat on the end of Onyx's bed with his hands in his lap. It had been on the tip of his tongue to argue—or at the very least ask what it was Onyx wanted. He'd pulled it back at the last second. He'd promised himself that he would stop trying to control everything, and this seemed like a good place to start.

When Onyx stepped through the door, Echo looked up at him with a smile but didn't move. Fiero had explained a few things about Onyx to him, and, though he was nervous, he wanted this. If it didn't work out, if he didn't like it, that was fine. He needed to try, though, needed to know if he had it in him to let someone else be in total control.

Onyx looked right into his eyes, crossing the room and kneeling on the floor at Echo's feet. His large hands rested on Echo's knees, and he rubbed and squeezed them absently. "Are you sure about this? You know what I'm asking from you, right?"

"Not everything, no, but I want to try. Will you be mad if I can't do it?"

Sadness settled in Onyx's eyes, and he shook his head slowly. "No, baby. I don't need this from you. I won't deny I want it—maybe more than I've wanted anything in a long time, but I don't need it. If you don't like it, say the word and everything stops. I won't be upset, and we'll just go back to the way things were."

"I want to try," Echo repeated. He wished he could give Onyx more assurance, but he was scared, and he had no idea what to expect. He really hoped that he didn't freak out and make a complete fool of himself.

"Then give me a safe word."

"Safe word?" Echo tilted his head to the side and his eyebrows drew together. "What's that and why do I need one?"

"It's any word you want it to be. I will never hurt you, but if at any time it becomes too much, you use your safe word. Everything stops immediately."

"Just like that?"

"Just like that, baby."

"Why do I need a safe word? Why can't I just say stop or no?"

Onyx seemed to consider his words for a long time before he spoke. "A safe word is unambiguous. What if I stop doing something you like, and you say no because you want it to continue? Or what if you ask me to not stop? Do you understand, baby?"

Echo nodded slowly. "What if I forget my safe word? Onyx, I've never done anything like this before. What if I mess up?" He was beginning to reach a new level of anxiety and seriously reconsidering if this was such a good idea.

"Shh, baby." Onyx reached up to caress Echo's cheek. "We'll start slow this first time, okay? Something fairly mild. If you like it, we'll go from there, okay?"

A little of the tension ebbed, and Echo sucked in a deep breath. "Do I still need a password?"

"Safe word, sweetheart, safe word, and yes. What if we use a color code at first—red for stop, yellow for slow down, and green for go? Would that make you feel better?"

Onyx was trying so hard, and Echo already felt like a total loser. They hadn't even started, and he was already questioning everything to death. "Please don't be mad if I mess up, or I don't like this."

"I promise. I told you, Echo, I don't need this from you. We don't have to do this if you're not comfortable."

"And it's just sometimes, right?" He didn't know why he felt he had to ask, but it seemed important.

"Right. With Hex being in charge around here, and me being in love with seven insanely stubborn men, it's not exactly conducive for everyday life. I do like having control. I like when my partners submit to me. It's more of a kink than anything else and does not extend outside the bedroom."

Echo knew this of course. How long had he been living there? Gods, he was making a complete fool of himself. Sitting up a little straighter and squaring his shoulders, Echo nodded firmly. "Okay."

Onyx stared at him for a long time before he finally dipped his head and rose to his feet. "Stand up." He voice was low, deep, and commanding.

Echo shivered, but rose to his feet instantly.

"You will not speak unless I ask you a direction question or to use your safe word. Do you understand?"

"Yes, sir." Echo didn't think he imagined the hungry look in Onyx's eyes when he addressed him as sir.

"Undress and place your clothes on the dresser."

Without a word, Echo slipped out of his clothes, folded them neatly, and laid them on top of the dresser. He moved back to stand in front of Onyx, his hands linked behind his back, and waited for his next directive.

Onyx didn't say anything, just turned and walked out the door. Echo hesitated for a moment, unsure if he should follow or not. He still didn't know the rules, but he hadn't been told to follow. Maybe Onyx expected him to just know? Gods, he couldn't do this.

"Echo."

A deep sigh of relief escaped his lips, and Echo hurried out of the room to find Onyx waiting for him in the hall.

"Follow me."

Onyx led him down the hallway, around the indented staircase that led up to the attic, and through a door behind it. The corners of Echo's lips tugged down in a frown. He'd been there for months and never noticed that door. Then his eyes widened when he stepped inside the small, dimly lit room.

Three tables were pushed against the wall, all displaying an arrangement of toys and objects—some he recognized, some he couldn't begin to identify. Another large table stood in the middle of the room, padded in black leather, with cuffs attached at each corner. A rather odd-looking swing hung from hooks in the ceiling.

There was a couch, an ottoman, and something that reminded him of the pommel horse that gymnasts used. There was also a wicked-looking contraption that brought to mind medieval torture devices. It stood tall in the corner of the room, leather cuffs attached to each corner, much the same as the padded table.

Crap, crap, crap! Echo's heart hammered inside his chest, his stomach rolled, and sweat broke out over his skin. He tried to take a deep breath but couldn't seem to pull enough air into his lungs. So, he breathed shallowly, sucking in oxygen as quickly as possible. Bad idea, he realized, when his head began to swim, and the room started to tilt.

A strong arm wrapped around his waist, catching him before he could crumple to the floor. Onyx swung him up in his powerful arms and carried him over to the sofa. He eased down on the cushions, settling Echo in his lap, and stroked his face gently.

"I'm sorry," he whispered. "Catch your breath, and we'll leave. I'll get you something to eat, we can watch a movie, whatever you want, baby."

Echo shook his head vehemently. "No. I can do this."

"You're pale, sweaty, and shaking like a leaf. You have nothing to prove to me, or whatever it is you think you're doing. I told you, sweetheart. I don't need this."

But, Onyx was wrong. He did need this. Echo had given himself completely and without reservation to his other mates. "I want to do this," he said firmly and pointed toward the door. "Outside that door, I'm too much of a control freak. I'll never roll over and just let you guys tell me what to do. It's not how I'm built."

Echo reached up and covered the warrior's mouth when it looked as though his mate would interrupt. "Sometimes, I just need to let go, not think, and allow someone else to be in control. And, sometimes, not always, you need to have that control."

Onyx curled his fingers around Echo's wrist and kissed his palm. "I don't want to always be in charge. I can't imagine having to make the decisions that Hex does. But, yes, sometimes I need that control. That's why I have this room. In here, I have final say. Things are however I want them to be."

"Then, I think we complement each other perfectly, don't you?"

A strange look played over Onyx's face that Echo couldn't decipher. He looked thoughtful, awed, and completely lost all at the same time. "I think you're right. Inside this room, we can give each other what we need."

Echo slid out of Onyx's lap and knelt on the floor in front of him, waiting.

"What is your safe word?" Onyx asked.

"Red for stop, yellow to slow down."

"Good, baby." Onyx reached down and caressed the side of Echo's cheek before standing and pulling Echo up with him. Onyx led him to the padded table and smoothed his hand over the dark, supple leather. It looked much bigger up close, somehow intimidating.

Echo moved to climb up on the table, but Onyx stopped him. Without a word, he pressed his palm between Echo's shoulder blades, urging him forward with gentle but firm pressure to his back. Echo bent at the waist until his chest met the cool leather, and he bit his lip to keep from groaning.

"Do not move," Onyx said sternly. He took each of Echo's wrists and moved his arms to stretch out in front of him on the table. Echo watched as Onyx crouched then stood straight again with a pair of velvet-lined handcuffs, one end secured to the floor with a thin chain. The other end locked around Echo's wrist, and then Onyx moved around the table to do the same to the other wrist.

Echo breathed slowly, in through his nose, out through his mouth. He could do this. Onyx disappeared, and it seemed like a torturously long time before he returned. Echo's body thrummed with nervous anticipation, practically vibrating as he waited to find out what Onyx would do to him next.

The demon's palms began smoothing over his skin, light caresses at first, then harder, more hungry as he kneaded the muscles in Echo's upturned ass. "So, beautiful," Onyx whispered. "You will not come until I give you permission."

"Yes, sir." It wasn't a direction question. Hell, it wasn't really a question at all, but Echo instinctively knew that Onyx wanted an answer.

"Good, baby," the warrior purred.

Echo's head popped up from the cushioned table, and he sucked in air through his teeth when cold liquid dripped over his skin and ran down his crease. The slight hiss instantly turned to a strangled groan before Echo could cut it off. One thick finger pushed between his ass cheeks, stroking his hole and coating it in lube. He wasn't sure if moaning counted as speaking, but he clamped his lips together just in case.

His fingers dug into the sides of the table in a white-knuckled grip when the slippery digit pushed into his quivering hole. Damn, it felt so good. He rocked back, arching his hips to take in more of the finger invading his ass.

A stinging swat landed on his left cheek, and Echo bit down hard on his lip to trap the whimper that rose up in his throat. "Be still," Onyx commanded.

"Yes, sir," Echo choked out.

One finger became two, two became three, and eventually Onyx had four long fingers pumping into Echo's clutching passage. Echo rolled his damp forehead against the table, his body quaking as he struggled desperately to keeps his sounds of pleasure locked inside. His dick swelled and pulsed, hardening almost to the point of pain.

Then his mate's fingers disappeared, replaced by something thick and unyielding. The silicone toy pushed inside his aching hole, and Onyx pumped the plug a few times before thrusting it deep into Echo's ass until the flat base pressed against the flushed skin of his cheeks.

Something soft, almost feathery drifted across his shoulders next, then down his spine and over his hips. It brushed over his bottom, up and down his crease, then disappeared. The next time it connected with his skin, it didn't feel feathery any longer.

A sharp sting lashed across his right buttocks, sending fiery heat shooting straight to his rock-hard dick. Onyx didn't stop with one, didn't even take it slowly. Over and over the flogger smacked against his bare skin. His hips, the back of his thighs, but it only occasionally struck against his ass.

"Your skin marks so well, baby. You should see how beautiful you look right now. Are you okay to continue?"

"Yes, sir," Echo answered shakily. His backside burned, but it was a good burn, and he wanted more.

Something flat and hard landed on his left cheek, and Echo tensed as he bit on his lower lip so hard that he tasted blood. That was definitely not a flogger, and it wasn't a goddamn hand either. The swats came slower this time, but with more intensity. Onyx paddled his ass, each strike harder than the last, until the muscles in Echo's ass actually began to twitch and throb.

The fire consumed him. His balls churned, his heart kicked hard against his sternum, and pre-cum leaked freely from the engorged crown of his cock. His nerve endings sizzled, and Echo didn't know how much more he could take before he went off like a bottle rocket.

It surprised him a little at how much he enjoyed the flogger and the paddle. He liked Vapre spanking him, but the warrior's hand had nothing on the sting of the leather that whipped over his skin. Nor had he even thought about the restraints until he'd gone to reach for his throbbing cock. His brain felt a little fuzzy, high, almost disconnected.

Another swat landed on his aching ass, and Echo's fangs shot through his gums, descending until they pierced his bottom lip. His throat began to burn, his mouth watered, and he sucked in air through his nose, trying desperately not to make a sound.

He certainly wasn't thinking anymore, though, and that's exactly what he'd wanted.

* * * *

By the time Onyx set aside the satin-lined paddle, his hands were shaking, his body quivering, and his cock throbbed painfully inside his jeans. Echo hadn't moved, other than the slight tensing and trembling of his body. He hadn't made a sound either. He was so proud of his baby.

Picking up the small bottle of salve, Onyx dipped his fingers in the goo and spread it gently over Echo's flaming skin. "You did so well, baby. How are you feeling?" When he didn't receive a response, Onyx began to worry. "Echo, talk to me."

He set the gel aside and moved slowly around to the side of the table to look at his mate. What he saw made his chest tighten and his heart bleed. He didn't think he'd lost control. In fact, he'd held back from what he'd have normally delivered to one of the warriors.

But Echo's eyes were squeezed closed, his face dripped with sweat, and he bit into his bottom lip so hard that blood trickled down his chin. Onyx had been overjoyed to hear Echo say that they complemented each other. He'd been waiting centuries to finally fit with someone. Oh, he knew his men cared about him, but he often found himself floundering, trying to find his place in the relationship.

Echo was his miracle. He'd come along just when Onyx needed him the most, and now he'd most likely screwed up everything. "Echo, open your eyes."

His mate's eyes snapped open immediately, and the heat, lust…the hunger blazing in his blue orbs, stole Onyx's breath. Echo's own breathing came in shallow pants through his nose while his lips pressed together firmly, his fangs glistening in the overhead light where they peeked out.

He skimmed the pad of his thumb over Echo's chin, wiping away the blood. "Baby, open your mouth."

Echo complied immediately, sucking in air in a giant gulp as his body began to shudder.

"Why didn't you use your safe word?"

"Green, sir," Echo replied huskily. "Please, sir. I need to come."

Onyx closed his eyes and groaned. Gods, his mate begged so nicely. He moved back behind Echo, pressing his denim-clad erection firmly against the toy still lodged in his lover's ass and reached around to palm Echo's weeping dick.

Echo's cock pulsed inside his grasp, the skin so hot and silky smooth. Onyx pumped him once, twice, then licked the back of Echo's neck. "Come for me, baby."

Just like that, Echo's body locked down, an almost silent groan fell from his lips, and hot seed splashed over Onyx's hand and wrist. With a satisfied growl, Onyx lifted his hand to Echo's mouth. "Clean me up."

Without hesitation, Echo's tongue snaked out, lapping that pearly cream on Onyx's fingers until he'd cleaned away all reminiscence. "Tell me what you want, baby."

"Fuck me, sir. Please," Echo panted.

"That's all?"

"I…I need…"

Onyx pushed the hair back from Echo's face and gripped his chin to turn his head to the side. "Tell me what you need, Echo."

"It burns," he whimpered.

"Here?" Onyx caressed his mate's heated ass lovingly.

"No." Echo shook his head. "I…I…my throat."

Enlightenment dawned, and Onyx hurried to release the handcuffs. Once he had his mate unbound, he scooped Echo up and carried him out of the room. "Why didn't you say anything?" he demanded.

"You told me not to speak. Where are we going?"

"Oh, baby, you did so well. I think that's enough for now, though. I'm going to take care of you."

"You already did." Echo's lips tugged down at the corners in confusion. "I need to take care of you."

Onyx's cock continued to throb inside its confinement, but the need for release had abated. The only thought in his mind, the only desire in his heart, was to see that his mate was well attended to before tucking him into bed. Not once in his entire life had he passed up a warm hole so willingly offered.

But Echo was different.

Walking into his bedroom, Onyx closed the door quietly behind him and went to sit on the foot of the bed with Echo still cradled against his chest. He stroked his lover's hair, his face, and trailed his fingertips over Echo's swollen bottom lip. "Take what you need, sweetheart." He tilted his head to the side, baring his throat to his mate.

A needy whimper reached Onyx's ears just before Echo struck, sinking his canines into Onyx's neck and sucking hard at the wound. His other hand zeroed in on Onyx's throbbing cock, squeezing and massage him through his pants.

Lightning strikes of overwhelming pleasure slammed into him, robbing the breath from his lungs, and Onyx groaned pathetically as his cock discharged, saturating his boxers and leaving a wet stain on his jeans.

His arms wound around Echo's back, holding him tightly, encouraging his mate to take as much as he needed. "I love you," he whispered.

If someone had told him a few short months ago that his entire world would change with the arrival of one beautiful little imp, he'd have laughed in their face. He'd be eating crow now, of course, but he'd do it with a smile on his face.

Yes, Echo was definitely his miracle.

Chapter Five

Myst pounced on Craze the minute the man walked into the kitchen. "Where have you been? Where's Jinx and Syn? Why didn't you tell anyone you were leaving? Why don't you want to talk about it? What happened?"

Hex chuckled and looped his arm around Myst's neck. "Give the man a chance to talk, babe." He kissed Myst's temple before releasing him and strolling over to take a seat at the table. He waved his hand for Craze to join him.

The other warriors gathered around the table as well, and Mac stood off to the side as though he wasn't quite sure if he should stay or leave.

Myst kicked the chair beside him out from under the table and gestured to it. "Have a seat, Mac. We'll figure out where your mates are, and we'll bring them home safe. I promise."

Mac gave him a tiny smile and slid into the seat beside him. "Thank you, Myst. I'm scared."

He ruffled the smaller man's hair and tried to drudge up some confidence that he didn't feel. "We'll find them," he repeated. The sad, lost look in Mac's eyes broke his heart. Sweet hell, he was becoming a total sap.

He blamed it on Echo.

Speaking of his mate… "Should we wait for Onyx and Echo?"

Vapre smirked. "We'll fill them in later."

"I'm pretty sure Echo is as about as filled as he's going to get." Fiero snickered at his own joke, and quiet chuckles went around the table.

"Okay, guys, can it," Hex chastised, but he, too, was smiling. Then he turned his focus back to Craze. "We'll get to you and your mates in a minute, but, first, do you know where Gage and Sony are?"

Craze's eyes darted to Mac, and his brow creased into a shallow *V*. "They're not here?"

Sliding further down in his seat, Myst groaned. How could six people go missing from their house, and no one knew where the others were? They all suddenly had something important to do at the exact same time?

"He's not answering his phone," Mac said quietly. "Do you think they left me?"

"Not a chance," Syx answered with conviction. "Gage and Sony love you, Mac. You know that. They'll be back, and then you can make them pay for worrying you." He winked at the man, but Mac didn't smile.

"I don't want them to pay. I just want them home."

Myst patted Mac's knee, but he didn't have a damn thing to say to reassure the runt.

"Okay, so where have you been, and why the fuck didn't you tell anyone?" Hex demanded of Craze.

"I'm sorry," Craze said coldly. "I didn't realize I had to report to you."

"Do not start your shit, asshole," Fiero called from his usual place at the end of the table. "We just want to know why everyone fucking disappeared. After the shit that's been going on around here, you can't blame us for getting a little bent out of shape. Now, answer the man."

"You swear too much," Echo chided as he walked into the room with Onyx close on his heels.

Myst eyed them both carefully, but couldn't find anything amiss. Sighing in relief, he turned his head up to meet Echo's lips when his mate bent to kiss him. "I'm fine," Echo whispered. "You worry too much, love." He rubbed their noses together before continuing around the table to greet each of the warriors. He went to Fiero last and tapped the end of the demon's nose with his index finger. "Don't curse so much. It makes you sound like a douche bag."

"Newsflash," Fiero said with a smirk. "I am a douche bag."

"Mmm"—Echo purred—"but such a handsome one."

Myst snorted and rolled his eyes. "Don't encourage him." He glanced over at Onyx, finding the man leaning against the kitchen doorway and grinning like a fool. Did he look like such a lovesick idiot when he looked at Echo? Probably.

Echo huffed when he couldn't find an available chair and settled into Eyce's lap. Eyce looked like he'd won the lottery, grinning cockily at them all. Myst rolled his eyes again. Some warriors they were. They might as well be baking cupcakes and singing to the woodland creatures when Echo came around.

Somehow, he couldn't find it in himself to care, though.

"Are Jinx and Syn okay?" Echo asked. He held up his hand when Craze turned an angry stare on him. "I'm not asking where you've been, or why you felt the need to skip out in the middle of the night. I just want to know if my friends are okay."

Craze deflated instantly. He slumped in his chair and rubbed both hands over his face. "I didn't tell anyone because there wasn't time. I woke up in the middle of the night and my mates were gone. I went after them, as any one of you would do."

Myst nodded his agreement. If he'd awoken to find Echo missing, he'd have destroyed everything in his path to find the man. "Did you find them?"

"Yes," Craze said through gritted teeth. "They've gotten it in their heads that everyone hates them because they bit Echo. I tried to talk some sense into them, but they think they need to make amends."

"So, where are they? Why did you come back without them?"

"Staying with them would only put them in more danger." All heat had left Craze's voice, and he just sounded like a scared little boy.

Myst had never heard that particular tone from Craze before, and it made his chest tighten. "Where are they?"

"I guess you know that Jet and Pax are with Lorcan?"

Everyone nodded.

"Jinx and Syn went with them. By the time I'd caught up to them, the coyotes had already let it slip about the freakin' bloodsuckers that are causing mayhem in town."

Myst snapped his attention to Echo, waiting for the little brat to admonish Craze for calling the vampires bloodsuckers. Echo smirked and shook his head. "It's okay to call *bad* vampires that, just not my friends."

"Stupid double standards," Myst mumbled under his breath.

"What do the new vamps have to do with your mates?" Eyce asked.

"Jinx and Syn have watched one too many spy movies." Craze growled for a minute before he shook his head and continued. "They're going to infiltrate the enemy's camp and gather information for us. Their words, not mine."

"And you just let them?" Echo's eyes widened in shock. "Are you nuts?"

"I didn't track them down until just before sunrise this morning. They'd already met with the leader about joining the coven."

"So?" Echo tilted his head to the side.

Syx sighed and reached over to squeeze Echo's thigh. "When vampires are initiated into a coven, they exchange blood with the coven leader. Once ingested, the leader will always be able to feel them, know where they are at all times."

"What if they want to leave and join a different coven?"

Syx shook his head. "There is no exit clause. Unless the coven leader dies, his underlings will always be connected to him."

"So, a coven will have the same leader forever unless he dies?"

"Yes." Eyce took up the explanation. "A member of the coven, or even an outsider, can challenge the leader for the right to rule. The fight is to the death."

Echo's mouth dropped open, and he looked back at Craze. "Go get them!"

"Baby, he can't. None of us can." Eyce caressed Echo's back. "We haven't figured it out yet, but there's a reason these vampires are here now, and it's not a good one. If Jinx and Syn have already been accepted into the coven, then we'll only put them in danger by going after them."

"You are demon fucking warriors!"

"You curse too much." Fiero lifted both eyebrows and held his hands up in surrender when Echo growled at him. "Never mind."

"We can keep them safe," Echo said firmly. "They need to come home."

"The coven will kill them before we could even reach them," Craze said sadly. "Apart from being able to know where his members are, a coven leader can also feel their emotions and read their thoughts."

"So, we don't tell them. We just go in, snatch them, and get the hell out."

"Maybe they can get some information," Hex said slowly.

Myst thought Echo was going to come over the table after the alpha. He probably would have if Eyce's arm hadn't wound around his chest to hold him in place. "You are not serious! If you won't help me, I'll go myself. Whether they mean anything to you or not, they're my friends. I'm not just going to leave them!"

Echo cast pleading eyes around the table, looking at Craze last. "Please. They're your mates. Even if you don't love them, you have to feel something for them. Help me."

Craze looked away, unable or unwilling to meet the plea in Echo's eyes. Myst looked down at the table as well. While he wanted take the sadness from his mate's face, there wasn't much they could do without risking the little bloodsuckers' lives.

"I want them back," Craze said quietly. "We need a fail-proof plan before we go in, though. I won't have them hurt because we fuck this up."

"Okay, everyone calm down." Hex groaned and massaged his temples with his fingertips. "They're not in danger right now as long as we keep our distance. I hope," he added under his breath, and Myst thought he might have been the only one to hear it. "Let's focus on finding Gage and Sony. Then we'll figure out how to get Craze's mates out of the mess they got themselves into."

"There are ten of us at this table," Echo said indignantly. "I don't see why we can't do both."

Myst loved the little shit, but sometimes he just wanted to strangle him. Instead of starting another argument, he rose from his seat and stretched his arms over his head. "It's late. Everyone is tired. Let's get some sleep, and we'll figure this out in the morning."

Hex shot him a grateful look. "That sounds like a good idea. We'll be able to think better after we've all had some sleep."

Echo wasn't appeased, though. He threw his hands in the air and jumped up from Eyce's lap. "Whatever," he growled. "I can't believe you guys." He pointed a finger in Craze's face. "Especially you! I'm going to bed." Then he stomped out of the kitchen, grumbling under his breath the entire way. "Alone!" he shouted once he'd disappeared into the living room.

"Do you think he meant that?" Myst looked around the table for confirmation. Why the hell was Echo so pissed off anyway?

"I don't know," Fiero answered, pushing to his feet and stretching as well. "I'm not going to his room, though. I like my balls right where they are."

Myst reached down to cover his groin and dipped his head. "Good point."

* * * *

Echo paced his room. He sat down on the bed. He paced some more. Finally, he wandered into the bathroom and showered. Then he returned to his room to pace again.

He was pissed, but more to the point, he was disappointed. When he'd gone missing, everyone in the house had come together to search for him. It didn't matter that he wasn't mated to Gage, or Craze, or any of the rest. They'd dropped everything and torn the forest apart to find him. Now that Jinx and Syn needed their help, everyone hesitated.

A soft knock on his door froze him mid-step, and he growled. "I meant what I said. I am sleeping *alone*!"

"Echo?" Mac's quiet voice drifted through the heavy wood, and Echo rushed over to unlock the door.

"Sorry. I thought you were one of the guys."

Mac waved away his apology. "I understand. I don't want to bother you, but well…I can't sleep by myself." He looked down at the floor, and his face flushed to the tips of his ears. "I'm really worried about them, Echo."

Echo rested his hand on Mac's shoulder and sighed. "I know. I am, too. You still can't reach Gage?"

"I found his cell phone under the bed," Mac whispered. "I don't think they're coming back."

"Stop it." Echo squeezed his friend's shoulder. "You know they're coming back. Mac, that letter that Gage left for you, did he specifically say that Sony was with him?" Echo didn't want to worry Mac any more than he already was, but he needed to know.

"No," Mac answered slowly. His eyebrows drew together and his lips pursed. "He just said that he would be back and not to tell anyone. Why, do you think Sony is in trouble?"

Mac was way more perceptive than anyone gave him credit for, including Echo. "I think it's possible. If something happened to Sony,

I can see Gage going after him. He'd want you to be safe, though." He wasn't just trying to blow smoke up the guy's ass, either. Something told him that was exactly what had happened.

"Do you think Sony left by himself?"

"I can't answer that. I think Gage did what he thought he needed to do in order to protect you both. They're coming back to you, Mac. Just have a little faith in your mates."

"Yeah, I guess you're right. Do you think Jinx and Syn are going to be okay?"

"I intend to make sure of it." Echo shoved his fingers through his long hair and growled. "I don't know why Craze didn't just drag them back here. We're strong. So what if they have some weird bond with this psycho coven leader? We can protect them."

"What if they can find out something useful? I know you're mad at Hex, but he's just thinking like a leader. Now, Craze, I don't get that guy at all. He gives me the creeps." Mac gave an exaggerated shudder.

"I don't like Craze very much, but that's just plain old jealousy. Maybe I'm missing something, or just not getting it, but I don't know why he left his mates if they're in so much danger. You'd think he would have at least stuck around close enough to keep an eye on them in case there's trouble."

"If Jinx and Syn had already been accepted into this coven…" Mac trailed off, and his thumb went to his mouth where he began chewing on the nail.

"Go on." Echo definitely wanted to hear where this was going.

"How did he talk to them? They said we couldn't get near them without the leader knowing. So, how did Craze get to them?"

"I don't know." Echo grabbed Mac's wrist and dragged him to the door. "We're going to talk to Hex."

Chapter Six

"You have been deceived, Warrior."

Onyx looked out over the grassy field and smiled. So this was what Elysium looked like. He wouldn't mind spending eternity in the place. The warm sun, the distant roar of waves crashing against the shore, the gentle breeze that brought the intoxicating scents of endless spring—he wanted it all.

"There seems to be a lot of that going around," he finally said. The Oracle no longer hid behind her long blond hair or willowy white gown. The goddess, Athena, stood before him, dressed for battle. "You have done quite a bit of deceiving yourself."

"I did what I could to help you. Would you have trusted me as I am now, knowing who I am, who my brother is?"

"Probably not," Onyx conceded. "So, why am I here?"

"I will not abandon you just because you now know my identity. I cannot give you all the answers, but I can guide you."

"So, who's lying?"

"Everyone."

"That's not really helpful. Can you be more specific?"

"Everything you have learned this past night has been lies. Ares seeks to destroy your army."

Onyx didn't know what to say for a minute. He hadn't really expected a more forthright answer. "So, the shifters aren't with Lorcan? Jinx and Syn have not joined forces with the evil vampire clan? Craze is a lying bastard?"

"The last is merely a fact. Not a lie." The goddess smirked at him.

"Why would Lorcan lie to us?"

"You ask the wrong questions, Warrior. Find the right questions, and the answers will be clear." Then she simply vanished.

What the fuck was that supposed to mean? Gods on Olympus, Athena, the Oracle, whoever she was, had to be the most infuriatingly unhelpful person who'd ever existed.

It was time to pay a visit to Syx's question board.

Onyx peered up at the stunning blue sky and sighed. Why couldn't things ever be easy?

* * * *

Loud pounding on the door jerked Onyx out of his fitful sleep. "Get your ass up," Fiero called. "Craze is gone."

Swinging his feet over the side of the bed, Onyx sat up and rubbed his stinging eyes. Blinking at the alarm clock, he realized he'd been asleep for no more than an hour. He was exhausted, confused, and downright irritable. "Coming," he called back grudgingly.

His eyes felt gritty, his brain disoriented, and he really didn't want to deal with this shit. Pushing off the mattress with a grunt, he grabbed a pair of sleep pants from his dresser and donned them quickly. With any luck, he'd find out what was going on and get his ass back in bed pronto.

Fiero stood just outside his door, his face red, and his lips pressed together in a thin line. "Craze has pissed me off for the last time. When I find him, I'm going to beat that asshole until he bleeds out on the carpet."

Just at the moment, Onyx agreed wholeheartedly. Still, maybe he should find out what was going on before he started beating people into submission. "What happened?"

"The fuck if I know. Echo and Mac come running into Hex's room, spouting off questions about how did Craze talk to the little bloodsuckers if it's so dangerous to go after them. They wouldn't shut up until we agreed to talk to Craze, but when we went to find him he was gone. Now Hex is pissed, Echo's screeching like a goddamn vulture, and I just want to crawl into a hole and sleep for the next year."

"Then I guess you don't want to hear about the dream I had?"

"No." Fiero shook his head. "I don't."

Onyx sighed and rubbed his palm over his short, dark hair. "Okay, let's get this meeting over with so we can get back to bed."

Once down the stairs, they marched side by side to the kitchen and took their places around the table without a word. When Onyx was seated, he waved a hand at Hex and blinked sleepily at him. "Athena says we're being deceived, and Craze is a rat bastard. She also said we're asking the wrong questions. There's my two cents, so what's going on?"

"I told you!" Echo yelled as he paced back and forth between the kitchen counter and the center island. "Don't you find it just a little too coincidental that Lorcan called when he did? Why didn't he call as soon as Jet and Pax arrived? And Craze is a lying sack of shit!"

"Don't hold back, babe." Fiero chuckled under his breath. "Tell us how you really feel."

"I feel like you better start taking this seriously, or I'm going to cram my fist up your ass and make your mouth work like a puppet."

Fiero continued to laugh. "Duly noted."

"I think we're looking at this all wrong." Syx frowned down at the glossy wood of the tabletop. "We've completed every task laid before us so far. Ares has to be getting desperate. What if this is just to distract us from the next test? If we're concentrating on finding all our missing houseguests, we're not focusing on preparing for what's coming."

"I can see that," Echo said slowly. "It doesn't matter, though. We can't just leave them."

"What if they're not really missing?"

Onyx snorted. "Are you listening to yourself?" He waved his hand around the kitchen. "Do you see them anywhere? They're not here.

We don't know where they are. In my book, that's the epitome of *missing*."

"That's not what I meant, and your shitty attitude isn't helping."

"Stop," Echo said quietly. "This is exactly what Ares wants. Us fighting each other and running around chasing our asses. Let's just take one thing at a time and go from there."

Onyx sucked in a deep breath and let it out slowly. Echo was right. "Come here." The relief was instant when Echo hurried across the room and crawled up in his lap. Onyx wrapped his arms around the man and kissed the top of his head, allowing the scent of his mate calm and soothe him. "I'm sorry."

Echo patted his chest and nuzzled against his throat for a moment before sitting up straight to address everyone in the room. "Okay, so let's start over. We know that seven members of this house are missing. We know that there are bad-guy vampires in town running amok."

"Amok, huh?" Vapre smiled brightly, his eyes shining with amusement.

Echo growled at him, and Onyx had to bite the inside of his cheek to keep from laughing. "Go on, Echo."

"Well, that's really all we know. We assume Jinx and Syn are with these vampires because of what Craze said, but his story had a lot of holes in it."

"We know that Jet and Pax are with Lorcan," Myst offered.

Echo shook his head slowly. "Don't you find it odd that Lorcan called right at the exact time that we were going to call him?"

"You're saying Lorcan is lying?" Hex frowned and rubbed more insistently at his temples.

"Not exactly," Echo hedged. "Someone convinced this Lexi person they were you and to transfer all that money."

"So, maybe this conveniently timed phone call came from someone other than Lorcan?" Syx bobbed his head thoughtfully. "Well, we can clear that up easily enough."

"On it," Eyce said, rising from the table and pulling his cell phone from his pocket. "Keep talking. I'll be right back."

"What did you mean about them not being missing?" Onyx asked again, though much calmer than the first time.

"I didn't mean that exactly. We think they all left around the same time, right? But we assume they all went in different directions. That doesn't really seem plausible."

"I'm still not following you." Onyx was beginning to understand why Hex had so many headaches.

"What if they didn't leave? What if they were taken? I mean, yes, they're still technically missing, but if they're all in the same place, we have a better idea of where to find them," Vapre tried to explain.

"And where would that be?" Fiero asked.

Before anyone could offer an answer, Eyce walked back into the kitchen from the living room, and the back door swung open. Everyone was on their feet at once, Myst pushing Mac behind him, while Onyx shifted to stand in front of Echo.

Craze looked at them all with wide eyes and held his hands up in surrender. "I just went for a walk to clear my head."

"Sit your ass down and start talking," Hex ordered. "You're lying, and I want to know why."

Onyx eyed Craze warily as the man came further into the room and sat down in the seat Fiero had recently vacated. He wasn't the only one either. They had no way to know if they could trust their ex-lover, and it made him twitchy. He didn't want Echo anywhere near the man.

Very slowly, everyone resumed their seats, Fiero snagging the chair beside Onyx and leaving Hex to pace. "If something happens to my friends because you're a lying fuckwad, I will gut you like a fish," Echo said calmly. "I promise you won't be able to heal from what I do to you. So, you have about two minutes to make this right and prove to me why I shouldn't do exactly that."

"I don't have a reason why you shouldn't, and to be honest, I wouldn't fight back."

"Explain," Eyce growled.

Onyx had never heard so much hostility in one word before. If Craze didn't start giving them some answers soon, things were going to turn ugly fast.

"Your story doesn't add up." Echo paced right alongside Hex. "If it's so dangerous for us to get to Jinx and Syn, then how did you talk to them?"

"I just talked to a member of Lorcan's pack," Eyce added. "Lorcan is missing as well, so it definitely wasn't him who called earlier. None of the pack have seen Jet and Pax either."

Craze propped his elbows on the table and dropped his forehead to his hands. He spoke without looking up. "I don't know about Lorcan, or any of the others. I swear, I don't."

"Then where are Jinx and Syn?" Myst asked icily.

"Exactly where I said they were." Craze finally lifted his head to look at them. His eyes were red-rimmed, and he swallowed several times before he spoke again. "I told Jinx and Syn about the vampire clan that moved into the area. I wanted them to be on their guard and understand why they couldn't go off on their own."

"So why did they?" Onyx asked.

"They were feeling guilty about attacking Echo. I should have just kept my stupid mouth shut!" Craze shook his head and pulled at his spiky blond hair. "I wasn't even thinking. I made some stupid comment about how it would be nice if we had someone inside the coven that could feed information to us. I was just thinking out loud, ya know? I fell asleep and when I woke up they were gone."

"When was this?" Hex paused in his pacing to face Craze.

"The same night as the new moon." Craze sighed. "I knew exactly where they'd gone, but by the time I got there it was too late. They'd already been initiated into the coven."

"Why didn't you just tell us that?" Mac fidgeted in his seat as he spoke.

"Because I fucking ran like a coward!" Craze yelled. "First I plant the idea into their heads, then I get there just in time to watch them being beaten and fed the blood of the coven leader, and I did nothing to stop it!"

"You didn't try to save them?" Echo asked incredulously.

"They were surrounded by thirty goddamn vampires! If I'da made a move, Jinx and Syn woulda been dead before I could reach 'em." The man's southern accent slipped in the more agitated he became. "I'm strong, but I ain't strong enough to face down thirty vampires. I hung 'round the next day, tryin' to figure out a way to get to 'em, but this clan is a lot bigger and a lot stronger than we thought."

"We would have helped you," Echo said, but he'd abandoned the scathing tone. "Why didn't you ask for help?"

"This is my mess," Craze snarled. "I didn' wanna drag y'all into it. I know y'all think I'm some big asshole, and Jinx and Syn deserve bettah. Yer prob'ly right. I have to get 'em back, though."

"You really don't know where Gage and Sony are?" Mac whispered.

Craze glanced over at the smaller man and shook his head sadly. He took a deep breath and looked to be trying to compose himself. "I'm sorry, Mac. I'd tell you if I did."

"We don't think this vampire clan showed up out of the blue," Onyx said slowly before looking to Syx and Vapre for help. Something niggled at him, but he wasn't sure exactly what. As the brains of the group, if Onyx could spark a thought for the two, maybe they could come up with the answers.

Instead of saying anything, though, Syx smiled at him and nodded. "Keep going."

"We think they're mostly likely connected to Ares."

"Right." Vapre nodded.

"So, these vampires would already know all about us." A light went off in Onyx's head, and he pushed up straighter in his chair. "They would know Jinx and Syn were there to deceive them."

"Exactly," Syx said. "Which leads me to believe they somehow used Jinx and Syn to lure the others out of the house."

"So, you think Gage and Sony are being held by these assholes?" Mac shot up from his chair. "No!"

"Yes." Syx growled and banged his fist down on the table.

"We have to get them!" Mac yelled.

"If they're as strong as Craze says, that's damn near impossible." Onyx looked away as he spoke. He didn't want to see the anger, desperation, or disappointment in Mac's eyes.

"I'm willing to bet they don't have just Gage and Sony, but Jet, Pax, and possibly Lorcan," Vapre snarled. "It's a trap, and they're using them as bait."

Chapter Seven

"When do we leave?" Echo knew his men would go. He knew their first concern would be for him. "It will take all of you to get them out, and it's not safe for me and Mac to stay here alone. We're coming with you."

"How long until sunup?" Hex asked. Echo was a little surprised that the demon wasn't going to argue with him.

Echo glanced out the kitchen window. "An hour, give or take." It still unnerved him that he could feel when the sun was rising. If he wasn't a vampire, then how did he know that? There were a lot of questions about this whole *daemon* thing that he needed answered. Shit just kept popping up, though, and he hadn't had a chance to even think about, let alone understand it.

"Our best bet is to go in during the day. Craze, do you know where they're being held?"

Crazed nodded and jumped to his feet. "Yeah, I can get us there." He took a deep breath and let it out in a rush. "Thank you."

Hex waved away the gratitude and focused on Echo. "Baby, we're going to need a lot of go-go juice. Do you think you can handle that?"

Go-go juice? Echo chuckled. "Yeah, I can handle it." Thank the gods his powers were still intact after dying. He shuddered a little but kept the smile plastered on his face. When was he going to get over that? He'd died. Big deal. It wasn't like he was buried in the ground somewhere. Still, the thought always left him feeling cold—no pun intended.

"Okay, then everyone suit up."

The warriors all moved as one, rising to their feet and leaving the room with Craze and Mac right behind them. Echo tilted his head to the side as he watched them go. "What are they doing?"

Hex smiled and brushed a stray lock back from Echo's forehead. "They're getting their gear."

"Daggers, swords, and black leather pants—like real warrior stuff?" Echo asked excitedly. The thought of seeing his mates decked out in leather and shiny blades should probably terrify him, but it didn't. It actually made his dick twitch inside his cotton pajama bottoms.

"Yep." Hex skimmed his fingers down Echo's chest and cupped his growing erection. "You like that, don't you?"

Echo licked his lips and moaned. "I think I like that a lot."

Hex wrapped his fingers around the back of Echo's neck and tugged him into a kiss that set his head spinning and his cock throbbing. They were both breathing heavily when Hex pulled away and released his hold on Echo's groin. "We'll play after we save the day."

Gripping his aching shaft through his pants, Echo groaned. "Cock tease."

"It's not teasing if I come through." Hex pecked him on the lips again and swatted his ass to get him moving. "Put some clothes on and meet me at the front door in ten minutes."

Echo was dressed and waiting in five. He fidgeted nervously, pacing back and forth in the entryway at the foot of the stairs while he waited on his mates to join him. When they finally emerged, Echo thought he'd swallow his tongue.

Hex wasn't kidding. They were all dressed in black leather pants and plain black T-shirts. Black boots and heavy belts adorned with an array of knives in different sizes rounded out the drool-worthy picture. They looked dangerous—and absolutely the sexiest men he'd ever laid eyes on.

Hex laughed and kissed him on the forehead when he reached the foot of the stairs. "I told you."

"Told him what?" Fiero asked.

"Echo seems to have a fetish for leather and knives," Hex answered with a smirk.

All eyes turned to him, and Echo swallowed hard. "I want to strip you down and lick every inch of each one of you." Good grief, he'd actually said that out loud. Shaking his head to try to clear a bit of the lusty haze surrounding his brain, Echo turned and reached for the doorknob. "This is going to be a distraction," he mumbled under his breath.

Hex's hand landed on the back of his neck and urged him around to face the big alpha. "No distractions," Hex said seriously.

Echo dipped his head. The magnitude of what they faced finally crashed down on him, and his knees began to tremble. "Don't you dare die."

Stroking his fingers down the side of Echo's neck, Hex frowned. "Where's your necklace?"

"Upstairs in my nightstand." Echo's throat burned at the hurt look in Hex's eyes. He curled his hand around his mate's wrist, moving the warrior's palm to his cheek to nuzzle against it. "I haven't worn it in a while. It's too important to me, and with everything happening, I was afraid it would get lost or broken."

His answer seemed to appease his lover, because Hex grinned crookedly and stroked Echo's cheek. "This is a two-way street, Echo. You will do exactly what we tell you to do, and no arguments. Not this time, baby. Don't you dare die." He growled Echo's words back to him.

Echo nodded, though he wasn't even sure if he could die anymore. Would he re-die? Was that even possible? It was definitely something he needed to find out, but this probably wasn't the best time to test it.

One final check to make sure everyone had what they needed, and they hurried out to pile into two separate vehicles. Echo slid into the backseat of his SUV between Onyx and Mac. Such a beautiful car his men had bought for him, and he'd only driven it once. He didn't much like driving, though, so he wasn't too fussed with it.

Hex drove as usual, with Eyce in the passenger seat. Everyone else piled into Syx's SUV and off they went to face down rogue vampires and rescue their friends. Cakewalk, right?

Echo fidgeted, squirming in his seat and wringing his hands together. So many things could go wrong and probably would. If all the vampires would be sleeping and they couldn't come out in the sun, how hard could it be? Judging from the amount of steel his mates were packing, he wasn't going to like the answer.

"I still don't understand why this is going to be so hard," he finally admitted. "I mean, we have powers, and the vampires can't come out in the daylight. Why is everyone acting like we're facing down Armageddon?"

"I imagine that they'll be holding Gage and everyone else in the lowest part of the building—a basement or something similar where sunlight won't reach," Eyce answered, turning in his seat to face Echo. "We have to get in, find them, and get out."

Echo nodded slowly. "But how hard could it be to kick their asses?"

"Craze said there were thirty or so vampires at Jinx and Syn's initiation. Which means there is probably double that in the coven. Vampires are fast, Echo. Yes, we have powers, but we usually need a moment to concentrate before we can use them. They won't give us that time. It's eight of us facing sixty or more of them."

"Nine," Echo amended. "I'm not just here to look pretty."

No one argued with him, but he saw the way Eyce's eyes tightened at the corners and knew his mates would do all they could to keep him out of the fray. Well, just let them try. He had no intentions of sitting on the sidelines while the men he loved put themselves in danger.

Watcher, daemon, angel, or whatever they wanted to call it, he was now faster, stronger, and his power was easier to manipulate. If he had to kick his mates' asses for their own good, well then so be it.

They sped along the dirt road that would lead them into town. Well, Echo assumed that's where they were going since he'd never actually been into the town before. No one said anything, and he was grateful that Syx had chosen to ride in the other vehicle. Hatching a plan would be damn near impossible with the demon listening in on his thoughts.

Echo stared down at his hands, concentrating with everything he had. He didn't know how he'd produced the bright light when he'd assaulted Gage in the kitchen that day. He did know it was powerful, though. He'd been trying to reproduce the glow ever since, but so far nothing. A crying shame, because he had an inkling it could be very useful against the vampires.

It felt like no time at all had passed when brake lights in front of them drew Echo's attention. The SUV pulled off the country road onto an even bumpier dirt trail and stopped completely. Hex pulled in behind Syx, pulled the emergency brake, and cut the engine.

"Are we here?" Echo looked at the trees surrounding them. He was really coming to hate the forests surrounding their home. Nothing good ever came from trekking out into the woods. And what about the town? Had he been lost in thought and missed it?

"You didn't expect us to just drive up to the front door, did you?" Eyce winked at him, his smile big and eager as though he was looking forward to the battle.

Echo guessed he probably was. His mates had been born for this. The last two thousand years of having nothing to fight had probably been wicked boring for them. He rolled his eyes and gave Mac a little shove to get him moving. "Let's go before Eyce wets himself."

Mac looked at him with wide eyes but hurried to scramble out of the vehicle. "Echo, I can't help," he whispered when they were both standing beside the SUV. "I *want* to help, but look at me." He spread his arms wide. "I'm just a human, and smaller than average at that. I can't fight vampires and win."

"No one expects you to," Echo said calmly. "Just stay behind the rest of us, and do exactly what we tell you. If someone tells you to run or hide, you do it. Okay?"

Mac nodded firmly. "I don't care about dying. I just want my mates back, and I don't want to fuck anything up."

"You won't." Echo grabbed his friend's wrist and pulled him toward Syx's vehicle. "Just don't say anything. They're going to try to talk us into staying, but it's not going to happen. Got it?"

"I'm not staying here." A rather impressive growl rumbled up from Mac's thin chest.

Echo had no intentions of being left behind. He wasn't above using whatever weapons he had in his arsenal to get his way, either. So, when Onyx called his name, instead of groaning like he wanted to, he pasted a winsome smile on his face and turned to his mate.

"Mac, would you please wait with the others? I need a word with Echo."

Mac looked at Echo for confirmation then nodded reluctantly when Echo waved him on. Stepping closer to the warrior, Echo kept the smile on his face. "Yes?"

"You need to feed."

The smile slid right off of Echo's face. He'd expected Onyx to argue with him and demand he stay behind. He even expected a little begging and bribing. This, however, he never saw coming. "Why?"

"Do you feel stronger after you feed?"

Echo thought it over for a minute. "Yes."

"You need to be at top strength, babe."

"Not you." Echo wanted to smack himself in the forehead when Onyx instantly shut down.

His entire body tensed and his eyes became shuttered. "I'll get one of the others," Onyx responded in a monotone.

"I didn't mean it that way." Echo grabbed his lover's wrist to prevent his escape. "I took blood from you last night, and a lot of it." He reached up and stroked Onyx's face. "You need to be strong as well, love."

Onyx's eyes softened, and he leaned into Echo's touch. "I'm sorry that I jumped to conclusions."

Echo didn't know what had happened in the demon's past to make him think he wasn't good enough for the love Echo felt for him, but once they rescued the others, he intended to change Onyx's way of thinking. The man never said much, but Echo guessed Onyx felt more than any of them. He was hurting, that much was obvious, and it broke Echo's heart that he couldn't take that pain away.

"I love you," he whispered. They were only words, but it was all the comfort he could offer in their given situation.

Onyx closed his eyes, his shoulders relaxed, and a contented sigh escaped his lips. "I love you, too." His eyelids fluttered open, and he smiled. "You still need to feed."

"If it will make you feel better. Though, I really don't think it's necessary. I just fed a few hours ago."

"It couldn't hurt," Onyx countered. He glanced over his shoulder toward the east. "We need to hurry."

The sky had lightened considerably since they'd arrived, and Echo could feel the tingle in his spine heralding the sun's journey toward the horizon. "Ten minutes or so," he mumbled. Gods, he was such a freak. He vaguely wondered if he could predict the weather as well. "I don't need to feed, and none of you can afford to give me the blood."

Onyx frowned at him. "It doesn't make me feel weak or tired. I think one of us could spare a little."

"No," Echo said firmly. "I'm good." He took Onyx's hand and squeezed it. "Let's go kick some vampire ass."

His mate gave in, just as Echo knew he would, and they hurried over to join the others. "Why do you have blankets?"

Craze looked over his shoulder at Echo, then out toward the eastern sky. "Jinx and Syn are vampires, Echo, and the sun is almost up. I'd rather not bring my mates home as charcoal."

Duh! Echo did smack himself in the forehead that time. Damn it, he needed to get his head on straight. "Right. Sorry."

"How far from here?" Hex asked.

"About a half mile through those trees," Craze answered, pointing toward the north. "It's a large house, a lot like yours. I couldn't get close enough to see inside, but all basements are underground."

"Do you know if there's an outside entrance?"

Craze shook his head and tucked the blankets under his arm. "Not a clue."

"I really don't want to go inside that house." Hex began pacing, his fingers clenching and relaxing at his sides.

Echo stepped in front of the alpha to halt him. "I think it's time for some go-go juice."

It didn't take long for Echo to go around the group, recycling and redoubling the demons' powers. He reached Syx last, unsure what to do. Maybe he should give Syx some of the others' powers?

Syx chuckled and kissed his forehead. "Don't worry about me, sweetheart."

Echo shrugged. *Right.* Like he wasn't going to worry.

"Hey." Syx slipped his fingers under Echo's chin and tilted his head up. "Look at me."

Echo did and yawned immediately. "I feel sleepy."

Chapter Eight

"Why am I sleeping?" Echo glared at the goddess, Athena. "This is bullshit! Send me back!"

"I did not do this to you, young one."

"Syx," Echo snarled. He should have known. Just wait until he got his hands on the asshole! "You can still send me back. They need my help."

"Yes, they do. More than they realize."

"You can say that again," Echo scoffed. "If I ask you some questions, are you going to be all mystical and vague?"

Athena arched an eyebrow at him and smirked. "It would depend on what questions you ask."

Echo shrugged. As long as he had the goddess there, he might as well try and get some answers. "Why did I die?"

"To fulfill your purpose," she responded immediately.

Yep, they were going to play solve-the-puzzle. "And what purpose would that be?"

"To win the war."

Echo growled. Maybe if he changed the wording a bit, he'd get better results. "So, you knew I would die? Why did Ares kill me?"

"So that you would not fulfill your purpose."

Echo had never wanted to throttle anyone more in his life. "Why doesn't Ares just strike us all down and be done with it?"

"He cannot." Athena actually laughed at this. "Father has bound his powers."

"So, he's not a god anymore?"

"Oh, he is still very much a god and will not be easily defeated. He may materialize wherever he chooses, or switch forms between man and wolf. No more."

"That explains why he's building an army and why he'd need to steal the money to fund it." Echo tapped his chin as he thought it over. Things were finally starting to come together. He still felt like he was missing something, though. Something dangling just outside of his reach. "Why does he want to go to war in the first place?"

"To prove himself and regain Father's favor."

"I thought he hated Zeus and vice versa."

"You should not put so much faith in human fairytales of the gods."

"Fair enough." Echo paced in the grass. "What part does Hades play in this war? We've all agreed that it doesn't make sense that he would be the one to issue these challenges."

Something flashed across Athena's face too quickly for Echo to identify it. "You will have the answers you seek when the time is right."

"What about their eyes? Why are my mates' eyes changing color?"

"The eyes are the windows to the soul, and only love will set you free."

"Did you really just quote clichés at me?"

Athena laughed, the same tinkling laugh she'd had when Echo knew her only as the Oracle. "It is time to wake up, my dear Echo. I do enjoy our visits, but your warriors need you. Remember," she said as she began to fade away, "true evil lurks in the shadows, too afraid to face the light." Then she was gone, and Echo was slammed back into his body.

With a quiet snarl, he flipped his eyelids open and bolted upright into a sitting position. Scanning his surroundings, he found Mac passed out on the ground beside him, but no one else in sight. Surely his men hadn't just left them there, asleep and defenseless.

"Damn it," a voice growled to his left, and Echo jerked around just in time to see two huge men step through the trees. He jumped to his feet, positioning himself between Mac and the newcomers, preparing to fight in their defense.

"I thought Syx said they'd sleep for a few hours?" the other guy asked.

"He did. This fucking blows."

"Who are you?" Echo demanded.

"Echo, calm down," the first guy said. "You don't remember me from your party? I'm Jason."

Flipping through his mental Rolodex, Echo tried to drudge up a memory of the man. "This is your mate, Oliver," he answered slowly. "You're from the coyote pack, right?"

Jason smiled and nodded. "We're supposed to keep an eye on you two until your mates come back."

"Well, I'm sorry, but I don't intend to make your job easy." Echo tilted his head to the side. "Is the rest of the pack here?"

"Just the sentinels," Oliver answered. "We came to recover our alpha."

"Well, I came to recover my friends and make sure that my men don't end up dead." Echo looked over his shoulder at Mac. "Keep him safe." Before either man could argue with him, he turned and sprinted through the trees, using his newfound strength to push him faster than he'd ever run before.

They called after him, but no footsteps followed, so Echo slowed when he burst through the tree line. A large, two-story house sat in the middle of the clearing. Craze was right. It did look very similar to their home.

Keeping close to the trees, Echo crept around to the back of the house, searching for a way inside. He didn't know how long he'd been asleep, but judging from the sun's position in the sky, it had been at least half an hour. How far would his mates have made it in that time? Was it enough time for them to find the others and get out? If so, where were they?

He didn't have to wait long for answers. He'd taken two steps away from the shadows when the double doors of the cellar burst open, banging loudly against the cement surrounding them. Gage had Sony thrown over his shoulder when he appeared, and Echo breathed a sigh of relief. The werewolf sprinted toward him, Jet and Pax following closely behind, both carrying identical bundles in their arms.

Jason and Oliver raced into view just as Gage reached Echo. The werewolf only spared him a passing glance as he rushed past him to deposit Sony in Jason's arms. "Keep him safe," Gage ordered then turned back toward the house.

Echo shoved past the shifters and ran with Gage. "Where are my mates?"

"Fighting," Gage bit out. "Go back, Echo."

Echo didn't waste his breath by arguing. He turned on a burst of speed, flying past the ex-guard and reaching the cellar entrance several steps ahead of him. He leapt down the stairs, taking them two at a time into the dimly lit cavern below.

The noise level was deafening. Snarls, growls, roars, and grunts rang out, bouncing off the concrete walls. The warriors were locked in battle with what looked to be at least thirty vampires. There was so much movement Echo couldn't tell, and he didn't bother wasting time to take an accurate head count.

He hurdled the bottom step just as a man came flying through the air at him. He side-stepped easily, watching in horror as the guy's skin began to blacken and smolder before his eyes when he landed in the patch of sunlight shining through the open cellar doors. The vampire screamed, a bloodcurdling cry that left Echo feeling sick and cold down to his bones.

Pushing away his shock and revulsion, Echo ducked and dodged bodies, working his way to the center of the fight. There were coyotes here, but he couldn't distinguish them from the vampires. Dropping quickly as a large man raced toward him, Echo swept his foot out, sending the guy to the floor where he rolled into the sunlight. The guy screamed just as his fallen comrade had and began to smoke and gurgle.

Well, that was one way to figure out who the bad guys were. Strong arms wrapped around his chest, hauling him off the floor, and Echo panicked for a just a second before Craze's rumbling voice sounded in his ear. "I'm going to find the coven leader. We can't let him live."

"Go," Echo yelled over the noise. "He's too important. He won't be here."

"Watch your back, Echo." Craze deposited him on his feet at the edge of the battle and ran toward the opposite side of the room, crumpling attackers to the floor as he went.

Crap! What the hell did he do now? Each one of his mates was locked in hand-to-hand combat with at least two vampires. They were so overwhelmed they couldn't even use their powers.

Echo sensed more than saw someone approach him from behind and quickly dropped to the floor, pivoting on one foot as he swept the other out once more. The moment the guy landed on the floor, excruciating pain ripped through Echo's back.

Sharp fangs pierced his skin, and the vampire didn't just bite him, he chewed on his shoulder, trying his best to rip away the flesh. Echo screamed, struggling to get away, but every movement lodged the bloodsucker's canines deeper into his flesh.

The warriors all jerked around as one, their eyes landing on Echo before ear-numbing roars ripped through the basement. In that brief moment of distraction, two vampires launched themselves onto Syx's back, clawing, biting, and ripping at him until he staggered to the floor.

A fear like he'd never felt descended over Echo, and the war cries from his men increased in volume. Wind roared into the basement with enough force to knock several people off their feet. A dozen more were frozen in place, poised in the midst of their attack.

The pipes that ran the length of the ceiling in an intricate maze began to groan and clang until they split open and water poured into the room, swirling with the wind and beating against anyone that stood in the way.

Fireballs flew through the air, one after another, careening into anyone who remained motionless for too long. The demons didn't seem to care if they attacked friend or foe. Their eyes held a crazed look, and they all began to shift.

The vampire on Echo's back released him with a terrified shout, and Echo slumped to the floor, watching the blood pool on the concrete below him. He didn't have time to just lie there, though. He needed to get to his men before the warriors ended up killing them all.

With a great deal of effort, he managed to push to his feet and stagger through the torrential storm Vapre and Eyce had created inside the cavernous basement. He'd made it only a few steps when the ground beneath him began to tremble and large cracks appeared in the floor.

Shit! Onyx was going to bring the entire house crumbling down on them.

Dropping his head and rounding his shoulders, Echo held his arm up to shield his face as he pushed forward through the wind and water. By the time he reached Syx, the entire room was creaking and shaking. The support beams groaned in protest, splintering as they began to buckle under the strain.

His mates had fully shifted by then, completely nude, their clothes shredded and whipping around in the storm. Hex tackled the nearest person he saw, taking him down easily and biting into his neck.

Echo had to find a way to stop this.

Falling to his knees beside Syx, Echo shook him roughly. "Syx!" he screamed over the roar of the wind. "Get up! Help me!"

The demon groaned, but he didn't move. Echo tried several more times with no success before giving up and pushing to his feet again. Fine. He'd just have to do this the old-fashioned way.

Marching across the room, he felt like he was moving in slow motion as he pushed against the wind. Eventually, he reached Vapre and shouted his lover's name. Vapre wasn't listening, though. His arms were spread wide, his head tilted back on his shoulders, and his eyes closed.

"Sorry about this," Echo mumbled under his breath. Then he doubled up his fist, cocked his elbow back, and drove his knuckles into Vapre's jaw.

Vapre's head snapped to the side then back just as quickly, a feral snarl falling from his lips. "Snap out of it!" Echo screamed. His lover took a menacing step toward him, but Echo stood his ground. "Goddamn it, Vapre, don't make me hit you again. I love you." He spun in a circle to encompass his men. "I love all of you, and I'm not going to let you kill us!"

No one paid any attention to him. Echo threw his arms wide as he bellowed in frustration. Bright, golden light erupted from his entire body, shooting out from his fingertips and bathing the dark room in its blinding glow.

It was over just as suddenly as it began, but when Echo looked back at his lovers, it was to find recognition in their eyes. They appeared a little confused and a whole lot afraid.

"Everyone out!" Hex ordered. "It's coming down."

Echo didn't immediately understand what was coming down until he heard the loud crack as one of the support beams gave way. His eyes widened, his heart raced, and terror filled his heart. They wouldn't make it out in time.

Hex snatched him up, so much larger in his demon form, and cradled Echo to his chest, charging through the room toward the stairs that would lead them outside. "Syx!" Echo yelled, practically climbing Hex's shoulder to find the demon.

Eyce lifted Syx easily, slung him over his enormous shoulder, and hurried after Echo and Hex. Echo didn't breathe a sigh of relief until they'd all made it safely out of the basement, though. He recognized several of the beaten and panting men surrounding them as members of the coyote pack, and he even saw Lorcan limping across the grass.

Echo rested his head on Hex's shoulder, rubbing his cheek against him like a cat seeking affection. Everyone who mattered had made it out safely.

His eyes snapped open, and he jerked his head up to look into Hex's eyes. "Craze! He's still inside!"

"I'm right here, Echo."

Craze appeared in front of them, covered in bruises, cuts, and a substantial amount of blood.

Echo swallowed hard. "Is that yours?"

Craze looked down at himself and shook his head. "No."

"Did you find the leader?" Echo figured it was a stupid question considering the amount of crimson covering the man, but he had to hear Craze say it.

Craze looked at him for a long time with hollow eyes that made Echo shiver. "My mates are free."

Before Echo could form a response, the house groaned again and loud crashes could be heard from inside.

"Let's go," Hex called in guttural voice. No one questioned him, and though probably inappropriate, Echo's chest swelled with pride that everyone had such respect for his mate.

"Are we safe now?" he asked quietly.

Hex held him tighter and nuzzled his cheek against the top of Echo's head. "We're safe for now, little one."

Echo understood the words Hex hadn't spoken. They had defeated one enemy, but many more would come.

Chapter Nine

"Did you see that?" Myst whispered to Hex as they sped back toward their house. The last thing they needed was to be caught in the vicinity when the vampires' hideout came tumbling down upon itself. "Did you fucking *see* that?"

"Yes, now hush." Hex took his eyes off the road for just a minute to glance toward the backseat where Echo slept in Eyce's lap. "He saved our asses."

"Well, try telling him that," Syx mumbled from beside Eyce. "He feels guilty."

"Why?" Myst spun around in his seat to look Syx in the eyes. His adrenaline was beginning to wane, and it left him feeling shaky. When was the last time any of them had allowed themselves to lose control like that? If Echo hadn't been there, he could only imagine what might have happened.

"He's thinking it's his fault I got hurt." Syx smoothed his palm over Echo's leg. "I was losing that fight before Echo ever stepped foot inside the basement."

"We all were," Eyce agreed quietly. "I couldn't fight them off fast enough. Every time I'd try to use my power, there'd be another flying at me, and I'd lose focus."

"Same here," Myst mumbled. Those damn leeches were fast. Once he'd dispatched one of them, two more would lunge for him. Just before Echo arrived, Myst had been having serious doubts about their ability to make it out of that basement alive. "I thought I was going to throw up my heart when I heard him scream."

"Very eloquent," Vapre said around a snort as he leaned forward from the third-row seat. "But I know what you mean. I completely lost it."

"I hate that he got hurt," Hex growled. "If he hadn't, though, I think we'd probably all be dead."

"Dude, he completely smoked those vampires. I have never seen anything like that." Myst stared at Echo's sleeping form in amazement. "What the hell was that?" Their little mate had practically exploded into a ball of light, and when Myst could see again, the vampires had been charred crispy.

No one spoke, and they all looked just as mystified as he felt. "Is Echo okay?" Hex asked instead.

"Yes," Eyce murmured. "He's sleeping, and the wounds have already closed." He stared down at the man in his lap with such tenderness, Myst had to swallow down the lump in his throat. "How he will deal emotionally when he wakes up is another question."

"He's tough." Myst nodded curtly. "He'll be fine."

Syx sighed and dropped his head back to the seat. "I don't think he'll be afraid of us if that's what you're worried about, Eyce. Before he fell asleep, the only thing he feared is that we'd blame him for what happened."

"So, what do we do now?" Vapre asked.

"We get ready for the new moon." Hex's fingers curled tighter around the steering wheel until his knuckles turned white. "We try to find some answers. So far, we've been lucky. I have a feeling that luck is about to run out."

Though he didn't say anything, Myst agreed. How long could they continue to outrun Ares? It seemed the god was always two steps ahead of them, and as soon as they overcame one problem, half a dozen more cropped up.

It didn't help that their numbers had just been reduced either. "How ironic is it that Jet and Pax actually ended up being mated to Lorcan?"

"Are we sure it's a good idea to leave them with the pack?"

Hex glanced over his shoulder at Syx. "I don't think we have a choice. They're grown men, and it just seems cruel to keep them from their mate."

"Do you still think Lorcan will help in the war?" Myst didn't know what a bunch of shifter pups were going to do against creatures of the Underworld, but they weren't in any position to turn away willing allies.

"He says they will," Hex answered slowly. "We need Jet and Pax. I don't know why exactly, but if they were sent to us, there has to be a reason. Lorcan isn't just going to let his men go off to battle alone."

"Jet and Pax were pretty damn insistent that they are going to fight." Eyce chuckled under his breath.

"I get why the shifters are staying, but why Craze and the little vamps?"

"Safety in numbers?" Syx shrugged. "Craze almost lost his mates once. What would you do to keep Echo safe?"

"Anything, even live with a bunch of mangy dogs."

Everyone laughed quietly as Hex pulled to a stop in front of the house. Damn, it was good to be home. Though it couldn't have been more than a couple of hours since they left, it felt like a lifetime. Myst wanted a shower, food, and a nap—preferably naked with his lovers. He probably wouldn't get much sleep that way, but he was willing to risk it.

* * * *

The scalding water beat against his shoulders and neck, washing away the dirt, grime, and blood. Onyx stared into the drain as the filthy water whirled around it and disappeared. He didn't want to see anyone. Didn't want to talk to anyone. Hell, he didn't even want to be there any longer.

He'd lost control. For the first time in centuries, he'd lost control and almost killed the men he loved more than his next breath. Gods, they deserved so much better than him. How the hell did he even apologize for something like that?

The shower glass slid open, and Onyx groaned at himself for forgetting to lock the bathroom door. He didn't turn, didn't care who was with him. If he just ignored them, maybe they would go away.

"We're not going anywhere," Syx replied quietly. The "we" caught Onyx's attention, and he glanced over his shoulder but only found Syx there. Whatever. It didn't matter.

Though he reminded himself that he didn't care to see any of them, some part of his heart ached in disappointment that it wasn't Echo who'd come to find him. He could only imagine what his little mate must think of him—and none of it was good.

"That's enough," Syx said gently as he reached around Onyx to turn off the shower. "Come with us."

Onyx didn't move. "I'm not very good company right now. Maybe we can talk later."

"It wasn't a request," Hex said from outside the shower. His voice was deep and commanding, the tone he adopted when he was more their alpha than their lover.

With a silent sigh of resignation, Onyx pushed past Syx and stepped out of the shower. "What?" he growled.

"We need to talk."

"Fine." Onyx stomped over to the door and wrenched it open. They had every right in the world to tear into him about what happened back in that basement. Couldn't they at least give him five fucking minutes to deal with it before they started, though?

Butt naked and dripping wet, he marched down the hall to his bedroom, threw the door open and did a face plant on his mattress. He was being a total dick, and he knew it, but damn it, he just couldn't deal with all the shit anymore.

"Are you done?"

With a frustrated groan, Onyx rolled over to his back and stared up at his mate. "Maybe."

Echo snorted. "You're being a dick."

Yeah, he knew he was. "I know. If everyone would just leave me alone—"

"You'd do what?" Echo lifted an eyebrow in question. "Sulk in your room?"

"Echo, I almost killed us all. How do you think that makes me feel?"

"Well, I just obliterated a couple dozen vampires, and I don't even know how I did it. How do you think that makes *me* feel?"

Okay, so the man had a point. Still, Onyx wasn't up Echo's ass, badgering him to talk about his *feelings* and use his grown-up words. If his mate wanted to pout, then he should be allowed to pout. See, he could be completely reasonable.

Without a word, Echo began to strip, and pissed off or not, Onyx's body couldn't help but respond. His cock swelled to hard and throbbing in a matter of seconds with each inch of creamy skin Echo revealed.

When his mate had divested the last of his clothing, he stood just out of Onyx's reach, his impressive cock jutting from its nest of closely cropped curls. Echo palmed his length, curled his fingers around the turgid flesh, and stroked slowly.

"You want some control back," he said in a calm tone that didn't match the scene currently playing out in the room. "I need to give over that control. Normally, I wouldn't say that sex can solve our problems, but this might be the exception to the rule."

Onyx nodded dazedly. He didn't give a shit why Echo was standing naked and hard in the center of his bedroom. Sitting up slowly, he reached out for his mate, frowning when Echo took a step away from him. He was not in the mood to be teased.

"Get over here," he whispered.

Echo shook his head, a mischievous light flashing in his eyes. "Make me."

Onyx pointed at the floor between his feet. "On your knees, Echo."

His mate moved fluidly, moving in front of Onyx and falling gracefully to his knees. His fingers linked behind his back, and he looked up with such an innocent expression, Onyx wanted to devour him.

Stroking his lover's cheek, Onyx smiled crookedly. "Good, baby." They were only playing. Neither of them desired a D/s relationship outside of the bedroom, but if Echo needed this, Onyx was more than happy to give it to him. "What do you want, Echo?"

"I want you to fuck me, sir."

The crude words falling from the lips of such an angelic face made Onyx's dick jerk as pre-cum dribbled from the slit and down the side of his engorged crown. "Then we have to get you ready." A game or not, painful pleasure or pleasurable pain, Onyx would never risk hurting his mate for anything.

"I already did that." The little imp actually winked at him.

Onyx reached down and swatted Echo's ass. "You are not being very submissive, baby."

Echo didn't say anything, but the corners of his lips twitched, and Onyx wanted to groan. The man was going to be the death of him. On the other hand, he'd completely forgotten why he'd been in such a foul mood only minutes before. His entire world centered around the golden-haired beauty on his knees in front of him.

Onyx bent forward and claimed his mate's lips, unconcerned with power play or the need to be in charge. He needed Echo. With that one thought, he laid siege to the man's mouth, licking inside the moist depths and moaning. His hands roamed Echo's pert ass, loving the feel of the soft skin beneath his palms. He squeezed and kneaded, gripping the rounded globes and pulling his lover closer as he devoured his sweet mouth.

So lost in the mating of their lips and tongues, Onyx didn't realize they weren't alone until the bed dipped and a wet tongue traced up the side of his neck. "Want you," Syx whispered in his ear, causing him to shiver.

Breaking the kiss, Onyx glanced up, unsurprised to find all six warriors standing around them, watching with heated gazes. He quickly amended his list of wants and desires. Yes, he needed Echo, but he realized that he needed all of his men. Something felt broken between them since the incident in that basement, and he needed to fix it before it caused a rift between them.

Whether they blamed him for his part in the collapse of the house or not, he blamed himself. He'd do whatever he needed to do to make it up to them. He couldn't lose this.

"Not losing anything," Syx mumbled, his plump lips sliding up and down Onyx's neck. "We'll talk later. Right now, I just want you to feel."

Oh, Onyx was feeling all right. His cock throbbed almost painfully between his legs, straining from his groin, reaching for his mate. Echo smiled, licked his lips, and dove forward to capture the leaking head between his lips. His tongue flicked and swirled. His teeth grazed gently along the sensitive flesh, and Onyx thought he'd lose his mind.

"Let us take care of you," Myst murmured seductively as he climbed up on the mattress on Onyx's other side. His strong hands roamed Onyx's body, smoothing down his chest and over his hip. "Let us love you."

Love. Onyx loved each and every one of these men. He didn't think Myst meant the word in the same context as he did, but he wouldn't argue. They wanted him, and he needed them with an intensity that clawed at his insides.

Suddenly, taking control, calling the shots, and dominating his lovers didn't seem quite so important. He held the power without even lifting a finger. Whatever they did to him, he allowed it, and that gave him the control he sought. So, why had it taken him so long to understand that?

Echo looked up at him, his lips stretched taut over Onyx's cock, and the answer seemed very clear. With trembling fingers, Onyx brushed the hair back from his mate's face as his throat burned with emotion. There would still be times when his playroom called to him. He'd still want that powerful feeling he felt when his men submitted to him. But he'd *want* it—not *need* it.

"Where have you been all my life?" he whispered down to Echo. The line would probably be cheesy and corny in any other setting, but Onyx spoke the words with sincerity. All the years of feeling out of place, and in a few short months, Echo had changed everything.

Instead of replying, Echo chose that moment to bury his nose against Onyx's groin and swallow around the head of his cock. All semblance of coherent speech fled, and Onyx dropped his head back on his shoulders and groaned deeply.

Syx and Myst continued to kiss and lick at his throat, tug at his pebbled nipples, and attack his senses. Fiero moved slowly to kneel behind Echo, touching every bit of their mate that he could reach. Echo moaned, the vibrations surrounding Onyx's cock and traveling down his shaft to burn in his tightening sac.

Syx and Myst eased him back to the mattress, pulling his spit-slicked cock from Echo's mouth so that it bounced up and slapped against his lower belly. Before Onyx could groan in protest, Myst moved to straddle his hips, holding Onyx's dick at attention and slowly lowering himself onto it.

Onyx closed his eyes, a feral growl rumbling inside his chest as he fought not to slam his hips upward and bury his aching shaft in Myst's tight heat. His knees were pushed wide, his feet moved to rest on the bed near his ass, and a wet tongue swiped over his fluttering hole.

"Oh, fuck!" Onyx lost his loose grasp on self-control and arched his back, driving his cock up into Myst's clutching passage. The warrior groaned, his eyes closed, and he gripped at Onyx's shoulders in a bruising hold.

Syx continued to nibble at his neck. Myst rose and fell over him, his inner walls convulsing in waves and massaging Onyx's cock until he thought he'd explode. The slippery tongue bathed his hungry entrance, lapping over the muscles, circling them, then pushing inside and wiggling around.

He sucked his lip between his teeth, biting it hard to keep the needy whimpers inside. Syx's thumb smoothed over his chin, tugging on it until Onyx's released his lip and turned his head to look at his lover. "Let it out, babe. We want to hear you scream."

Onyx growled, wrapped his fingers in Syx's sandy-blond hair and jerked him forward to devour his mouth. Syx moaned and writhed, his fingers digging into Onyx's pectorals when Eyce stretched out on the bed behind him. Syx's body bucked, his hips jerking forward to grind his steel-hard cock against Onyx's hip while Eyce thrust into his willing ass.

Up and down, over and over, Myst jackhammered his hips, pushing Onyx closer and closer to the edge. A thin finger slipped into his waiting hole alongside the velvety tongue, and Onyx finally realized it was Echo who licked and probed at his entrance. One finger became two, two turned into three, and eventually Echo had four fingers sawing in and out of Onyx's needy ass.

"Please," he whimpered, breaking the kiss with Syx. It was a strange sound to fall from his lips, but he couldn't care less. He needed release. He needed more. He just flat-out *needed*!

Echo's fingers disappeared, replaced by something hard, slick, and vibrating. The toy pumped into his ass in slow, languid strokes at first, then built in speed and intensity. Then Myst stilled, a strangled groan falling from his panting lips, and Onyx felt those slim fingers push into Myst's hole alongside his cock.

Two fingers slid over his pulsing length, stretching Myst's guarding muscles tighter around his cock. "Ready?" he heard Echo whisper a moment later.

Myst nodded eagerly, leaning forward so that his slick chest pressed against Onyx's. The digits vanished, and Onyx peered over Myst's shoulder at Echo's flushed face. His mate's eyebrows drew together in concentration as he stared down at the place where Myst and Onyx's bodies joined.

Then slowly, so slowly, the head of his cock slid over Onyx's shaft, nudging Myst's hole and rocking against it until the crown popped through the muscles, and Onyx nearly came on the spot. The dildo continued thrusting in and out of his hole, and he vaguely marveled at his mate's coordination. Myst groaned again, his body vibrating, and his fingers clenching and relaxing around Onyx's shoulders.

Echo continued to feed his long length to Myst's channel, his cock pressing against Onyx's until he pushed in as far as he could go. They stilled for just a moment until Myst demanded movement. "Gods, please, just fuck me," the demon begged.

The look on his face was a mingled combination of pleasure and pain, and Onyx began to have doubts that Myst was really enjoying what they were doing. Then Echo began thrusting, just small, minute movements, and the top of Onyx's head nearly came off.

Myst moaned, the sound one of pure pleasure, and Onyx's worry faded away. He stroked Myst's sides, his back, dug his fingers into the warrior's hair and slammed their mouths together demandingly.

"Big dick fucker," Echo growled, his movements stilling completely.

Jerking out of the kiss, Onyx looked down the length of Myst's back, his eyes almost rolling back in his head when he saw Fiero standing behind Echo, snapping his hips forward to drive his cock into Echo's sweet ass. Every thrust Fiero made, sent Echo's cock further into Myst's passage, and Onyx had no choice but to hold on for dear life.

Syx captured his lips again, but not before he watched Vapre step up to the side of the bed, fisting his hand in Myst's hair, and push his cock through the demon's parted lips while Hex drove into his ass from behind.

The strangle hold on his dick, the silky tongue sliding against his, the toy plunging into his channel—the sounds and smells—everything combined to set Onyx's heart thundering inside his chest and electricity spreading through his body. He could feel every bump, vein, and ridge of Echo's cock gliding over his own while Myst's channel convulsed around both their lengths and wet heat splashed against Onyx's chest and abs.

"Ah!" Syx moaned, his body stilled, and pearly ropes of cream shot from his slit and onto Onyx's hip. How big of a freak did it make him that he loved the fact that his men were branding him with their seed? Maybe Echo was onto something. Their little mate seemed to enjoy it immensely.

"Holy fuck!" Echo cried, and molten lava coated Onyx's cock.

Sweet hell, he'd never felt anything like it. Locking his arms around Myst's back, he slammed up into his lover and roared loudly as his orgasm ripped through him, and he filled the warrior's ass to overflowing with his semen.

Several groans went around the room, and Vapre was the last to find his completion. He pulled from Myst's mouth, leaned over the bed, and jerked his cock quickly. His eyes fell closed, the cords in his neck strained, and his chest rumbled when pearly cum erupted from the crown of his cock, falling in a graceful arch to cover Onyx's cheek and lips.

"That is fucking sexy," Myst breathed before he and Syx set to work licking Vapre's cum from his face.

His brain felt woozy and muddled, and maybe that's why he couldn't stop the next words that slurred from his mouth. "I love you, all of you." Onyx didn't even have time to worry about his lovers' responses before he closed his eyes and fell into a peaceful sleep.

Chapter Ten

Myst gasped and his heart stuttered as he scrambled off of Onyx and stood at the side of the bed. Hex had told him, Echo had said the words, but hearing Onyx profess love for all of them left him feeling shaky and vulnerable.

He probably made quite the sight, standing there flushed, with cum dripping out his ass, and his mouth hanging open like a goddamn guppy. It wasn't right, though. Onyx shouldn't just drop a big bomb on him like that when he wasn't prepared to deal with it.

"I never thought he'd be the first," Syx said with a slight groan as Eyce pulled his softening cock from Syx's ass.

"I didn't really either," Echo agreed. "I'm glad it was him, though. It seems right."

"It does." Hex bobbed his head.

"What the fuck are you talking about?" Myst stumbled back a few steps. This didn't appear to be news to anyone else, so why did he feel like he was scrambling to keep up? "The first one to do what?"

"To finally admit that he loves us all," Vapre answered calmly. "What else?"

"So, you all knew?" Myst stared at his men, understanding coming to him quickly. "You…you all…and you told…but me." Gods, that had been the epitome of lame. Before he could pull himself together and try again, though, Echo flew into his arms and squeezed him tightly.

"We all love you, Myst. It's scary a little bit, ya know? No one wanted to freak you out until you were ready to hear it."

"I've been ready for centuries," Myst admitted. It had been so damn hard to keep his feelings locked away inside. Now everyone was just spouting pretty words of love and loyalty, yet no one had bothered to inform him of the new rules.

"Well, my big, bad warrior," Echo purred and rubbed against him. "How are we supposed to know that? Did you ever tell anyone?"

"Hex," Myst whispered, and his cheeks flamed crimson. "Hex is safe."

"And what about me?" Echo asked softly. "Am I not safe? You know how I feel about you."

Myst mouth dropped open in shock, and he quickly gathered Echo into his arms and nuzzled against his throat. "Oh, baby, no, no, no. You know I love you. How could you not know that?"

"Well, you never said," Echo replied around a giggle.

Myst knew how much Echo hated to giggle, but gods, he loved that sound. "Well, I'm telling you now, little one. I love you. I love you so damn much that it hurts."

Echo kissed his temple before craning his head around to look at the others. "I'm waiting."

Smiles spread over the demons' faces, and they all murmured words of love to their mate. Echo huffed and wiggled down out of Myst's arms. "That's not what I meant, you big idiots. This has gone on long enough, and I want you all to admit that you love each and every one of us right now." He crossed his arms over his chest and stamped his foot.

Myst had to bite the inside of his cheek to keep from laughing. The brat was too adorable when he got himself into a snit. "I love you," Myst said very clearly, his eyes traveling around the room to include everyone. "I have loved you all for more years than I can count, and I, for one, am just fucking relieved to finally be able to say it."

Now that he'd spit it out, laid his heart at their feet so to speak, it didn't seem quite as terrifying as it had a moment ago. The looks on his men's faces told him that whether they returned the words or not, it didn't change what was inside their hearts.

"Ditto," Fiero said gruffly.

"Amen!" Vapre shouted.

"Agreed," Eyce and Hex said together.

"It's about fucking time," Syx grumbled, but he was smiling so wide, Myst thought his face would split in two.

"Glad I could help," Onyx mumbled sleepily, and everyone burst into laughter.

Echo squealed, throwing himself across the room and tackling Onyx back to the mattress when the man went to sit up. Myst thought he might actually prefer that sound to his mate's cute little giggle.

As he watched his men kiss and hug, Myst wondered why they'd all waited so long in the first place. Then Hex sashayed over to him, smirking the entire way, and pulled Myst into a brief but scorching kiss. "Love you, babe."

Myst sighed. This is how it was supposed to be.

* * * *

"Your eyes are really pretty." Mac batted his lashes and made kissy faces at Myst.

"Shut up," Myst growled.

A few snorts escaped the warriors, but Echo didn't hold back. He threw his head back and laughed with the sheer joy of it. "He's right, Myst. They're very pretty."

"They're fucking purple!"

"I'd say more lavender," Echo argued with a smirk.

"Isn't that purple?" Syx asked.

"Well, yes, but lavender is prettier."

Everyone jibed Myst for a few more minutes until Hex put a stop to it and called them all to order. Leave it to their alpha to ruin their fun. "Okay, so we need to debrief."

Echo stood up and reached for the button on his jeans.

"What are you doing?" Fiero frowned at him and reached over to still his hands.

"Hex said to debrief." Echo looked up innocently at Hex, but inside he was roaring with laughter at the look on the demon's face.

"Sit down." Hex sighed and scrubbed at his face. "Fucking brat," he mumbled under his breath. "Gage, tell us what you know."

Gage shifted on the love seat and pulled his mates closer to him. Echo didn't think the werewolf had let go of them since they'd arrived home. "The night after the new moon, I came downstairs to get a glass of water, and found Jet and Pax preparing to go for a run. They were still upset about what happened and how they'd attacked everyone."

He spoke calmly, almost as if he were on autopilot. Echo supposed it was better than the explosion he figured would come later.

"I'm sorry about that, by the way," Gage added. "Unlike Jet and Pax, I understand that I couldn't control it, but I hate that anyone got hurt." A little emotion had returned to his voice, and Echo tensed, waiting for the yelling to start. Gage continued calmly, though. "I told them to give me a minute to leave a note for Sony and Mac, and then I'd go with them. I'm sure they can take care of themselves, but I didn't think it was a good idea to let them go alone." Gage shrugged.

"Good thinking," Hex agreed. "What happened after that?"

"Well, I left a note saying that I'd be back and not to tell anyone I'd left. It wasn't some big secret, but I didn't want anyone to worry and come looking for us. That would put us all in a vulnerable position. Besides, I figured we'd be back within a couple of hours."

Mac groaned and covered his face. "I thought you meant not to tell anyone period. I thought you left me."

"I'm sorry, Mac." Gage kissed the top of his mate's head. "I wasn't thinking. I should have told you the reason I was leaving, but I was kind of in a hurry and not thinking."

"How does Sony come into all of this?"

"I woke up to see Gage leaving the room, so I followed him." Sony sat up straight as he took over the narrative. "When I made it downstairs, I heard voices outside, so I went out to look. Gage and the shifters were talking to Jinx near one of the cars."

"He said he'd heard noises in the trees and wanted backup to go check it out," Gage said with a slight growl to his voice. "I didn't even see Sony until we'd reached the tree line."

"Then what happened?" Echo marveled at Hex's calm authority. He was only hearing the story secondhand and his heart raced, thudding hard against his sternum. Hex looked almost bored, however. Echo knew better, but he still felt amazed that his lover could shut down his emotions like that.

"We got jumped by about twenty vampires and had our asses handed to us." Sony took a deep shuddering breath. "The next thing I knew, I was chained to the wall in some basement."

Hex looked to Gage for confirmation, and the werewolf nodded. "That about sums it up."

"So, Jinx betrayed us?" Echo's eyebrows drew together, and he frowned. He didn't know the vampire that well, but it just didn't fit with the man he'd been living with.

"No." Gage shook his head firmly. "I thought so at first, too, until I witnessed what happened in that basement."

"What happened?" Echo whispered. Gods, did he even want to know?

"Apart from bringing in a new person every day to change over, sometimes as many as four at a time, they are changing a lot more than humans."

"Don't you mean *were*?" Onyx asked.

"I don't believe we killed them all," Gage argued. "Not by a long shot."

"We know they kidnapped members of the coyote pack, but who or what else besides humans?"

"I don't have a roster for you, Hex, but I do know they have at least two skinwalkers."

"Fuck!" Hex spat, and loud groans went up around the room.

Echo tilted his head in confusion, mirroring the same look Mac was giving everyone. "What's a skinwalker?"

"They're usually witches," Syx explained. "You know how Jet and Pax shift into wolves, or Lorcan shifts into a coyote?"

Echo nodded mutely.

"Skinwalkers can shift into other humans, vampires, werewolves, whatever they want pretty much as long as they have the blood of whomever or whatever they want to look like. They literally walk in another's skin."

Echo reached up to cover his mouth as he gasped. "How do we know who to trust?"

"I hate to do this, but we're going on lockdown. No one leaves the house until we figure this mess out." Hex pushed up from the armchair and began pacing the room. "How long will our supplies last before we need to restock?"

"With five of us gone, I'd say at least until the new moon," Vapre answered immediately.

"Okay, so we have a little over three weeks." Hex seemed to be working something out inside his head. "If anyone comes to the door, they do not get in, got it? Not even if it's Craze, Lorcan, or any of the others."

Everyone nodded their agreement. What else were they going to do? Hex was right, and they all knew it.

"How is Onyx supposed to practice his power?" Eyce asked. "He needs to be outside for that."

Well, hell, Echo hadn't even thought of that. It seemed so much happened between each new moon that Echo always seemed to forget that the Big Bad was coming. They just fought a horde of freaking vampires. To him, that should count for something, and they could just skip the new moon and whatever challenge it brought. Of course, that wasn't going to happen, but a guy could dream.

"We'll figure out something," Hex replied distractedly. Echo could practically hear the gears turning in his head.

"Let's just figure one thing out at a time," Onyx suggested. "I think I'm going to have more time like Eyce did. It's not like dying crops are going to kill people overnight."

Echo figured the man had a point, but somehow he didn't think they were going to battling back grub worms with pesticides.

"Are we done?" Onyx asked.

Hex nodded. "I think we've covered all we know for now."

Onyx rose to his feet and crooked a finger at Myst. "You volunteered?"

Myst bobbed his head eagerly and jumped up from the couch. The minute he stood in front of Onyx, his entire demeanor changed. His shoulders went back, his head bowed respectfully, and he linked his fingers behind his back.

"You know what to do. I'll be there in a minute."

"Yes, sir." Then Myst hurried up the stairs.

Echo opened his mouth to say something but snapped it closed at the last minute. He'd thought Onyx had moved past what had happened earlier that morning. Obviously not. Why Myst, though? Had Echo not met Onyx's standards? Was he lacking something that made him a good partner for Onyx's games?

Onyx knelt on the floor in front of him as though he'd read every thought in Echo's head like it had been written out in bold letters across a marquis. He took Echo's hands and squeezed them gently. "We'll play again soon, okay? Myst needs this," he whispered quietly.

"Myst?" Okay, now Echo was even more confused.

"It's not my place to talk about it." Onyx placed a tender kiss over his knuckles. "This isn't about me thinking you can't handle what I like, okay? I can see what you're thinking, and don't. I'm more than happy to share my little world with you whenever you need it."

Need. Not want.

Echo nodded slowly. He was beginning to realize that he didn't know his men nearly as well as he thought he did. There were so many hidden depths to them, things they kept locked away in a secret place.

He wanted in. He wanted to break the locks on those places closed off to him, but did he even have the right? Everyone was entitled to some secrets. Right?

Then why did he suddenly feel like something was missing? Like a huge hole had opened up in his heart.

Plastering the best fake smile on his face that he could, Echo nodded like he understood what was going on. "I have something to tell everyone when you come back." He didn't much feel like talking about it right then, though. In fact, he didn't feel like talking about anything.

Chapter Eleven

Echo eyed Myst curiously when he and Onyx stepped into the downstairs office a few hours later. The demon looked more relaxed than he had earlier, but they all did. There was nothing conclusive in the way Myst moved or acted to clue Echo in to what had happened between the pair. Well, he had a good idea of *what* had happened. He just didn't understand the why of it.

It would have to be filed away to take out and examine later, though. "I had a dream."

All conversation and movement stopped instantly. "What dream? When?" Syx asked from his chair behind the desk.

Echo glared at him. "When you knocked me out this morning."

Syx didn't even have the decency to look ashamed of his actions. "I was trying to protect you. I'm only sorry that it didn't work like it was supposed to."

"Whatever." Echo waved his hand around in dismissal. It wasn't as though he expected a different answer. Put in Syx's shoes, he'd probably have done the same. To be honest, he'd been seriously considering asking Syx to put Mac to sleep. No, he really expected nothing less from his mate. "Anyway, about my dream…"

"Was it the Oracle…Athena?" Eyce dropped down to the cushions of the sofa and draped his arms over the back. "Did she give you more riddles?"

"Actually, I think I might have something that will help. I don't know exactly what it means, but you guys might."

"Do we need to get Gage in here?"

"It probably wouldn't hurt. I'd rather not have to repeat myself."

Myst bolted out of the room, returning only minutes later with Gage, Mac, and Sony filing in behind him. Myst gave them all a wide grin and went to settle on the sofa beside Eyce. "See, I have my uses."

Echo frowned. "You have a lot of uses, Myst."

The warrior's smile softened. "I didn't mean it that way, and me and you are going to talk later."

That sounded a little ominous for Echo's comfort, but what was he going to do? Tell the man no? So, he did what anyone would do when faced with something they didn't want to deal with. He ignored it. Maybe if he ignored it long enough, it would disappear.

"So what's up?" Gage asked, leaning back against the wall and pulling Mac to his chest. Sony leaned against Gage's side, looking happy as clam. Echo imagined the trio had a lot to be happy about.

"We're waiting on Echo to tell us." Hex looked at him and lifted an eyebrow. "So, spill it."

Pushing away everything else, Echo concentrated on remembering his conversation with Athena. "I asked her why I died," Echo began, pausing when his mates winced. Yeah, it sucked, but they were all going to have to get over it eventually—including him. "She said to fulfill my purpose," he finished.

"Wait!" Syx leaned forward in his chair and rested his elbows on the desk. "She knew you were going to die? I mean, it sounds like that was the plan all along."

Echo had thought the same thing. "Well, I don't guess it matters now, and I'm not dead anymore, so we're not going to worry about that."

"Okay, go on," Hex said tightly.

"Well, believe it or not, I did get some straight answers from her."

Everyone perked up at this, sitting a little straighter and staring at him intently. "No shit?" Fiero asked.

Echo rolled his eyes at the demon's word choice, but otherwise didn't react. "I don't know why Ares has lost favor with Zeus, but that's what this war is all about. He's trying to regain his father's approval, I guess." He let everyone chew that over for a minute before continuing. "Also, you're going to love this—he's lost his powers. Zeus has bound them in some way."

"Which is why he needs an army," Vapre said, catching on immediately.

Beaming from ear to ear, Echo nodded. "He can materialize and change into a wolf, I think she said, but that's it."

The men in the room seemed excited about this piece of information. Echo was pretty damn elated as well. They were finally getting somewhere. "So, I guess that in some ways explains the lab. I'm still not sure how it all ties in, other than the fact that he needs men to fight in the war."

"That would also explain why there are not women in the compound." Eyce curled his fingers around the back of Myst's neck and massaged gently as he spoke. "It has nothing to do with Ares being honorable, either. He just thinks women are inferior, beneath him."

"Well, that's stupid." Echo huffed when everyone turned to look at him skeptically. He held his arms out to his sides and twirled in a circle. "Just look at me. I'm no bigger than a woman, and smaller than some. Just because I have a dick doesn't make me any better, stronger, or more skilled."

"No one is disagreeing, babe." Hex moved over to him and kissed the top of his head. "We're just explaining why Ares would want men instead of women. I think it goes back to his rivalry with Athena."

"Because Zeus likes her better?"

"I don't know all the details, but I would imagine that has something to do with it."

Echo nodded. He supposed that made sense. Some men were just chauvinistic like that. "I don't really know much about women," he admitted. "They seem pretty fierce, though."

The men in the room nodded their heads solemnly. "Did Athena say anything about Hades?"

Echo turned to look at Fiero and dipped his head, paused, and shook it. "I asked about Hades. She got this weird look on her face and just said that I would have all the answers when the time was right."

"Weird how?" Eyce asked.

"I don't know, just weird. I guess almost afraid, but more…" Echo trailed off, his brow wrinkling as he tried to put an emotion to the expression on the goddess face. "I guess she looked kind of guilty?" He didn't mean to say it as a question, but he wasn't a hundred percent sure that he was interpreting his memory correctly.

The guys chewed this over for a minute, but no one appeared to have any answers. "Anything else?" Hex asked eventually.

Echo glanced at Gage, Mac, and Sony. He wanted to talk to his lovers about why their eyes had changed colors, but it was a conversation best had in private. He didn't see the importance of it in relation to the war either, so they could probably hold off on discussing the topic for a bit longer.

"Well, if that's all for now, we need to have a little word with Echo," Onyx said, pushing to his feet and motioning for Myst to join him.

"I didn't do it," Echo responded immediately.

The room erupted into laughter, and Echo bit his bottom lip and blushed. Onyx walked to the door and opened it, waving Myst through then crooking his finger at Echo. "Come along, little one."

The deep, commanding tone in Onyx's voice brooked no argument, and Echo found his feet moving before he'd given them permission to do so. "Yes, sir." He couldn't stop himself from falling right into the role he knew Onyx wanted him to play.

"Much better," Onyx murmured silkily. He slapped Echo's butt and nudged him through the door. "You have been very bad, baby." Onyx smirked at him as he pulled the office door closed. "Go to my room."

* * * *

Following Echo up the stairs, Onyx's eyes locked on the man's pert little ass. Damn, he was one lucky guy. Not one, but seven insanely gorgeous men loved him. He'd never done anything in his whole miserable life to warrant the affections of someone like Echo, but that wouldn't stop him from soaking up every bit of happiness he could get his hands on.

"Okay, really, what did I do?" Echo asked when they stepped through the door of Onyx's bedroom. He went and sat on the end of the mattress beside Myst and bumped their shoulders together. "You want to explain to me what this is all about? And should I be naked for the lecture?"

Onyx chuckled under his breath and shook his head. "No one is getting naked just yet. You have questions, so ask them."

"Why?" Echo blurted. "You said that Myst needed something from you. I don't understand." He looked at Onyx as he spoke then cast his eyes to the side to include Myst. "What do you need from each other that you can't get from the rest of us?"

Deciding it would be better to show Echo than try to explain with words, Onyx walked over to the bed and took his mate's hand. "Stand up."

Echo popped up off the bed like he had springs on his butt. Taking Echo's vacated seat, Onyx point to the floor between his and Myst's legs. "On your knees."

Just like that, Echo made a graceful descent toward the floor and knelt in front of them, his hands resting on the tops of his thighs. Onyx could see the confusion in his little man's eyes, but waited for Echo to ask his next question.

"Why did I just do that?"

Myst reached down and stroked Echo's creamy cheek with his fingertips. "Because you're tired of being in control. You don't want to think anymore. You don't want to have all the answers, or even pretend that you do."

Their mate's brow wrinkled further and his button nose scrunched adorably. "I guess that's true. I'm so tired of always being brave." He sighed dejectedly and his shoulders slumped. "My brain hurts from thinking so much. I know I'm supposed to help, be this great, infallible weapon in the war, but I just want someone else to take care of all that and tell me what to do." The corners of his lips twitched. "Well...sometimes."

"Now imagine that you were a three thousand year old demon warrior, born from the Underworld, and your only purpose in life is battle." Myst continued to stroke Echo's cheek, and the pad of his thumb drifted over the man's plump lips. "I don't always have the answers, and I don't always want to, Echo. Sometimes I just need to forget that all this exists and let someone else take over. Otherwise, my brain would probably explode."

"It's a bit of the opposite for me," Onyx tried to explain. He'd spoken some about it with Echo before, but he didn't think the little man truly understood it yet. "No one expects me to have the answers. Hell, I don't think anyone expects much at all from me." He ignored Echo's frown and Myst's low growl. "Hex is in charge, and everyone else seems to have their place in the group. Every day I deal with shit that I have no control over and it just eats at me."

He hoped like hell he wasn't just talking in circles. It was hard to put his feelings and needs into words, but Echo watched him intently, so Onyx continued. "I need a way to take back some of that control occasionally. I have no desire to lead us, and I don't mind being dominated, either. When things get to be too much, I need a way to take back that control, or I start feeling like I'm falling apart."

Echo stared at him for a long time before he finally shook his head. "If that's all it was, you wouldn't have felt the need to explain it to me twice. I don't know if you're trying to convince me or yourself, but I'm not buying it. Not all of it anyway. There's more to it, Onyx. I know there is." He turned his eyes to Myst. "Same goes for you. What are you two leaving out?"

Reaching out to cup Echo's other cheek, Onyx rolled his eyes at his lover. "You are too perceptive for your own good. However, I'm not leaving anything out—not anymore. For a long time, that room was my solace, the one place where the men I loved actually *saw* me. When I was in control, dominating them, putting them at my mercy, they paid attention, knew who I was, and really looked at me."

"We always looked at you," Myst whispered.

"I know that now, babe." Onyx leaned over and ghosted his lips across Myst's. "You and Hex have a special connection, same as Syx and Vapre, as well as Eyce and Fiero. I was never jealous, but it was hard not knowing where I fit."

"With us," Echo said firmly. "You fit with all of us."

"I get that now. I'm just trying to answer your question the best I know how. I can't change the way I felt, but I also think things are different now. Plus, I have you. You fit with me, and I'm not the odd man out anymore."

Echo nuzzled into his palm and purred. "I'm glad I found you."

"Not nearly as glad as we are." Myst bent at the waist and placed a chaste kiss on Echo's forehead. Then he sat back and sighed. "I don't really have any hang-ups. I just like being able to let go and not think or worry for a while. I also like that bite of pain that comes with being paddled or flogged. It lets me step outside of myself, and all I can do is feel."

Onyx winced as Myst fudged the facts a bit. He didn't like lying to Echo, but they weren't his secrets to tell. He guessed it wasn't technically a lie. Myst had just left out a few crucial details. "Everyone goes to the playroom at some point in time, baby." Onyx pulled his hand back and rubbed it over his short-cropped hair. How much did he tell his mate? "I think me and Myst just need it a bit more often than the others."

"So, what's your story?" Myst arched and eyebrow and smirked at Echo. "You are such a little hellcat most of the time. You don't take shit from any of us, and you're usually the first one to start barking orders or coming up with a solution."

Echo shook his head. Onyx could tell from the look on Echo's face that the little man knew he was only getting part of the story. Instead of making a big deal out of it, though, he went on to answer Myst's question. "I guess the same as yours. Onyx gave me a taste of what it's like to step outside my comfort zone, and I like it. Like I said, I can't be brave all the time. I can't be the answer man for everything. With Onyx—in that room—I don't have to pretend I'm either of those things."

"Baby," Myst sighed. "No one expects you to know everything, and we damn sure don't expect you to be fearless. This is some fucked-up shit we're facing. We're all a little afraid whether we want to admit it or not. There's nothing wrong with that."

"We are a messed up trio, aren't we?" Echo rolled his eyes, but his lips stretched into a wide smile.

Onyx supposed they were. Then again, every man in the house had some type of quirk that made him just a little insane. It made life interesting at least. He didn't need to dominate his men for the same reasons anymore, but that didn't mean he wanted to give it up all together. Luckily, he didn't think he'd have to—not if the wicked smirk on Echo's face was any indication.

"So, can we get to the naked part now?"

Onyx laughed in spite of himself before he could rein it in. He sobered quickly and adopted a low, demanding tone. "Go to the room, remove your clothes, and pick a paddle and a toy. Place them on the padded table then kneel on the floor until I get there."

Echo cast his eyes down, but his body trembled visibly in his excitement. "Yes, sir." He pushed to his feet and hurried out of the room without a backward glance.

Myst fell against Onyx and laughed when they heard Echo's footsteps running down the hallway toward the attic stairs. "He's eager, isn't he?"

Onyx sighed. "He's perfect." Now, he just had to work out Myst's issues before the demon imploded on himself.

Chapter Twelve

The next two weeks flew by, the full moon passed without incident, and still, tension hung heavy in the air of their home. They were no closer to discovering what Onyx would face, let alone how he would walk away victorious.

They'd spent a lot of time in Onyx's playroom, Echo needing the grounding and sense of well-being it gave him to turn over his control. The closer the new moon crept, the more he craved the stability Onyx gave him.

But they only had ten days to prepare for the task ahead, and Hex still refused to let anyone out of the house. Winter had finally let go of its stranglehold on northern Montana, giving way to the first warm days of spring, and Echo couldn't even go out and enjoy it.

"Damn it, Hex! He has to practice. If it's that big of a deal, everyone can come out with us. You're being completely unreasonable."

"You do remember what happened to Gage and the others, right?"

"It's the middle of the goddamn day! If everyone is together, I'm pretty sure we'll notice if there is two of someone. It's not like I'm asking to go to California. I just want to go out in the backyard!"

"Nothing has happened since we wiped out the vampires," Eyce reasoned, opening the refrigerator and extracting a bottle of beer. "I think if we all stick together, it'll be fine. Like Echo said, we'd realize if there were two of us."

"And what if Jet comes strolling along while we're out there? How do we know it's him?"

"How do we know it's him if he rings the fucking doorbell?" Echo wasn't trying to be an asshole, but he was damn frustrated, and their dear alpha wasn't making a bit of sense. "Hex, please. Everyone has been cooped up in this house for weeks. I'm just asking for an hour out in the sunshine. That's all I want. You'll be right there to protect me if anything happens." Echo sashayed up to his lover and stroked his chest—much the same as he was stroking his ego. "You'd never let anything happen to me, would you?"

Hex sighed and wound his arms around Echo's back. "You fight dirty, and you know I'd never let anything hurt you. One hour, Echo. That's it."

"That's all I'm asking for. Thank you, big guy." Echo turned his face up and puckered his lips for a kiss.

Hex chuckled, but bent and pressed their mouths together. "You are trouble."

"I try." Echo winked and spun out of his lover's arms to go find Onyx. He didn't have to look far, though. The big demon strolled into the kitchen just as Echo was rushing out, and it was like colliding with a freaking brick wall.

"Easy there." Onyx's hands gripped Echo's shoulders to keep him from toppling over. "Where's the fire?"

"Hex said we could go outside!" Echo beamed at him, bouncing up and down on his tiptoes like a child on Christmas morning.

"Oh, we got permission." Onyx cast Hex a scathing look, but deflated almost instantly and smiled back at Echo. "Then let's not waste it."

"Eyce, tell Gage that no one gets in this house until we're back. If someone shows up, he's to let us know immediately."

Eyce dipped his head curtly at Hex and took off to find the werewolf.

"I agreed to this as long as we stay together." Hex lifted an eyebrow at Echo and waved a hand toward the kitchen entryway. "Go find the others."

"Guys!" Echo bellowed. "Get your asses in the kitchen!"

Onyx rubbed at his ear and winced. "Sweet hell, you've got a set of lungs on you."

"All the better to scream your name, my love."

Ten minutes later, everyone assembled in the field behind the house. Echo turned his face up to the sun, delighting in the bright rays that heated his face. He really hated winter. If there was even the slightest possibility that they would go to rest in Elysium one day, he wanted it. Even in his dreams, the place was a beautiful paradise, and his heart beat rapidly with the thoughts of roaming those fields for the rest of eternity.

A silly dream perhaps, and probably not practical, but he couldn't help what he wanted.

When he finally opened his eyes, he found all seven demons staring at him with soft smiles on their faces. He'd be lying if he said he didn't enjoy the attention and the knowledge that he could bring that look to their faces. If something as simple as watching him enjoy the sunshine made them smile, he wasn't about to complain.

"So, what do we do first?" Onyx stepped forward and held a hand out for Echo. "Do you want me to move the trees? Maybe make the grass grow again?"

"Nope." Echo took his lover's hand and looked out toward the tree line. "I want you cause an earthquake."

Hex choked, coughing and sputtering while Eyce beat on his back. "You want to do what?"

"Hey, it could come in handy." Echo shrugged. "I don't think the prophecy meant crops in the literal sense. Even if Athena did mean the harvests, I seriously doubt they're going to die from drought or toxins. So far we've faced tangible beings. It only stands to reason that this won't be any different."

"I love it when he talks all smart." Myst winked and blew Echo air kisses when he glared at the warrior. "Love you, snookums."

"Oh, kiss my ass." Echo stuck his tongue out before returning his attention to Onyx. "I'd kind of prefer if you just gave us a little tremor, nothing too big."

"Yes, because I can control that," Onyx scoffed.

"You can." Echo squeezed Onyx's fingers and closed his eyes. "You have the power, babe. Now, stop being so pessimistic and just do it. Close your eyes and hold on tight." He didn't give the demon a chance to protest before dropping all his shields and sucking Onyx's power into himself.

He let it build and grow, filling him and recycling through his body, then pushed it at Onyx like a locomotive. What would have taken him several minutes before his *transformation*, now took mere seconds, and Echo found himself panting at the energy that coursed through him.

Onyx cried out, and his fingers wrapped around Echo's hands convulsively as the tendons in his neck strained. The warrior dropped to his knees, gasping for breath and sweating, before turning his head and heaving up the contents of his stomach.

"Shit!" Echo dropped down beside him and caressed the back of his neck. "I'm sorry, Onyx. It got away from me."

"I'm okay," he answered shakily as he pushed to his feet and stood on wobbly legs. "I just feel like I got struck by lightning."

Echo bit his lip and looked down at the ground. Not since he'd first had the idea of redoubling their gifts had he allowed his own to take over him like that. He didn't even know he'd done it until it was too late and Onyx was on the ground puking up lunch.

"Echo, I'm fine," Onyx assured him. He shook his arms and legs out, rolled his head on his shoulders, and cracked his knuckles. "Okay, everyone stand behind me."

Without a word, everyone moved several paces behind Onyx. Syx wrapped his arm around Echo's shoulders and pulled him close. "Stop beating yourself up, baby. He's fine."

Echo gave a noncommittal shrug of his shoulders and moved away from his mate. This close to the war, he couldn't afford mistakes. Zapping the shit out of the man he was supposed to be helping definitely counted as a mistake in his book.

Before he could get himself too worked up or depressed, the ground beneath his feet began to vibrate. It started as just a faint trembling, and Echo almost thought he imagined it. Then it began to grow, rolling across the earth in waves, and toppling Echo backward.

Fiero caught him before he could fall on his ass, holding him tight to his muscled chest. Echo beamed as though his firstborn had just been given a Nobel Prize. He really didn't understand why they all insisted they couldn't do these things. They had great power—only their confidence was lacking.

As suddenly as it began, the movement of the earth ceased. Onyx dropped his arms to his sides and turned slowly to give them all a shit-eating grin. "How was that?"

"Brilliant!" Echo exclaimed. "I told you, didn't I?"

"You did, but I still don't see how it's going to keep anything from dying."

"What exactly can you grow this far north anyway?" Echo tilted his head to the side in question. The ground had only recently thawed. Surely that wasn't enough time to plant seeds and produce yields.

"There are a four farms east of here in Flathead County that produce mint," Vapre offered. "I guess less than a thousand acres per farm."

"When's the growing season?"

"I think April through August, but I'm not really sure."

"How the hell can you grow anything here?" Echo demanded. "How can crops even survive with the snow we've been having?"

Vapre and Syx shared a quick look before both turning back to Echo. "I think these snowstorms have been isolated," Syx said at last. "There have been a few pieces on the news about it, even."

How sad was it that news like that didn't even affect him anymore? Echo rested his hands on his hips and shook his head. "Flathead County is too far from here. Everything has happened right on our doorstep. We'll have to keep looking for answers."

"Like Echo said, what if it's not literal?" Myst scratched the back of his neck and looked around the group. "Maybe the harvests or whatever aren't going to die, but it's meant to warn us against something that could cause that."

Vapre gaped at the warrior for a whole minute before wrapping his arms around him and swirling Myst in a circle. "You are a fucking genius, babe!" Then he planted a loud, smacking kiss on Myst's lips, dropped him to his feet, and sprinted toward the house.

Syx swiveled his head back and forth between the group and Vapre's retreating form, then gave a little wave and took off after the demon.

"I don't know why everyone is always so surprised," Myst mumbled under his breath.

"Because you're more apt to cause trouble than fix it." Hex chuckled and cuffed Myst in the back of the head. "You have great ideas, but you hardly ever voice them. It's nothing personal, Myst, and no one thinks you're stupid." Hex pulled the man closer and kissed his temple. "Love you, yeah?"

Echo's heart felt like it would burst with happiness. His mates had taken to expressing their love for one another with barely a hiccup. Every once in a while he would see one of them stop and shake his head as though he couldn't believe what he'd just said. It happened less and less over the weeks, and Echo went back and forth between smug satisfaction and wanting to knock them all upside their heads for denying it for so long.

"Ten bucks says Syx and Vapre have already found something," Eyce said a moment later.

Echo grinned brightly. "Make it a blow job, and you're on."

"You got it, darlin'," Eyce drawled. "If I win, you get to suck my cock. If you lose, you get to suck my cock."

Echo nodded, then stopped and frowned, his eyebrows drawing together in confusion as he worked the words around in his head. If he lost…and Eyce won, that meant—"Hey!" He jerked his head up to argue, but Eyce was already sprinting toward the backdoor. Echo crossed his arms over his chest, stuck his bottom lip out, and pouted.

The remaining demons howled with laughter, clutching at their sides and falling against each other like a bunch of damn fools as far as he was concerned.

Eyce didn't even make it to the back steps before Vapre came bursting through the kitchen door again with Syx hot on his heels. "Stymphalian birds!"

"Um, bless you?"

Vapre snorted at Echo as he jogged up to the group and thrust a piece of paper out for everyone to see. "The Stymphalian birds are sacred to Ares. Their dung is toxic."

"Eww." Echo wrinkled his nose. He took the sheet of paper from Vapre's hand and began reading the printout. "Man-eating birds with bronze beaks and metal feathers that can be shot at their enemies," he mumbled. "Well, that sounds just lovely. No big deal, right? It should be a walk in the park. I mean as long as we don't get eaten or impaled on flying feathers, everything is cool. Yeah, yeah, we're good." Echo could hear himself babbling, felt the hysteria bubbling up inside of him, but he couldn't stop. He continued on and on, repeating the same things in a variety of different ways, but all with the same undercurrent—They were fucked.

"Does this mean he's not going to suck my cock?" Eyce mumbled just loud enough for Echo to hear.

Hex growled and shoved at the man, but Eyce's words finally broke through Echo's panic, causing him to laugh. "Don't worry, love. Your pecker is safe with me."

"My pecker?" Eyce lifted both eyebrows and looked down at his groin. Then he looked up and shrugged. "You can call it whatever you want as long as it gets me a blow job."

"Asshole," Echo huffed under his breath, but he couldn't stop the grin that spread over his face.

"I don't know about that one. It would be kind of hard to put my asshole in *your* asshole."

Echo blinked at the man twice before doubling over in laughter. He laughed so hard his entire body shook, and he found himself on the ground with his arms wrapped around his midsection to hold himself together.

Myst huffed, and his next words only caused Echo to laugh harder. "And, everyone thinks *I'm* an idiot."

Chapter Thirteen

Onyx dominated, controlled, showed no mercy, and took no prisoners. One arm wrapped around Echo's lean waist, holding him in place as he drove into his lover's tight heat with a savage intensity.

His other hand fisted in Echo's hair, pushing his head forward so that Eyce's cock pushed to the back of their mate's throat. Eyce leaned back on the padded table, bracing himself on his elbows as his head dropped back on his shoulders.

Echo's arms were spread wide, handcuffed to the corners of the table, his fingers curled around the sides in a white-knuckled grip. He was completely helpless, totally dependent upon Onyx and Eyce to give him what he needed. The mere thought of it sent Onyx's shaky control on a downward spiral.

"Fuck!" Eyce roared a moment later, and Onyx pulled Echo back by his hair so that Eyce's hot, sticky release painted Echo's face.

"Please," Echo begged. "More. I need to come."

"You'll come when I say you can," Onyx growled and gave a sharp thrust of his hips to punctuate his statement.

Echo's head dropped forward on his shoulders, his fingers flexed and relaxed around the edges of the table, and his inner walls squeezed Onyx's cock in a vise grip. He moaned and whimpered, pushing back against each invasion as much as he could. "Please, Onyx, please."

Oh, his baby begged so beautifully. Onyx's cock swelled further, pulsing inside Echo's snug hole as he slammed in and out of the gripping passage. "Again, baby."

"Please, sir. Please let me come."

Eyce chose that moment to find his bearings, lean forward, and start licking his seed from Echo's face. The sight, combined with the delicious sounds falling from his mate's mouth, sent Onyx leaping over the edge.

Moving his grasp from Echo's hip, he palmed the man's bouncing erection and stroked him quickly. "Then come for me, baby." The words were guttural, snarled, and Onyx couldn't resist the temptation that the creamy skin over Echo's neck presented. Covering his lover's back, he felt his canines elongate as he trailed his tongue up the side of Echo's throat.

His balls drew tight to his body, aching and screaming for relief. Electricity hummed throughout his body, his head swam, and all he could think about was making Echo his all over again. "Mine," he growled just before sinking his teeth into the supple flesh and moaning like a whore.

Echo screamed, his inner walls clamped down on Onyx's throbbing cock, and warm, wet seed erupted from his slit to bathe Onyx's hand and wrist. Onyx lost all hold on his control and fell right over the cliff after Echo, emptying his balls into his mate's silky channel.

"Wow, I needed that," Echo panted.

Onyx extracted his fangs from Echo's neck and chuckled quietly. Easing out of Echo's quivering hole, he placed a soft kiss over his mating bite and nuzzled against Echo's throat. "Thank you." Then he reached over his mate, wrapped his fingers in Eyce's hair and urged him forward into a tender kiss. "And thank you."

Eyce smiled dopily at him before kissing Echo's temple. "Trust me when I say it was my pleasure."

Working together, Eyce and Onyx released Echo from his constraints, rubbing his wrists gently over the red marks on his skin. Though Onyx loved seeing the red lashes from his hand or crop on Echo's ass, these unsettled him. "I don't think we're going to use handcuffs anymore. Padded or not, I don't like this. You pull too hard on them."

Echo laughed and turned to wind his arms around Onyx's neck. "It doesn't hurt, and they'll fade away in a couple of hours. Can I help it if you drive me out of my mind, and I forget myself when you do all those naughty things to me?"

With a resigned sigh, Onyx brushed his lips over Echo's forehead and held him close. "You are the most manipulative little shit I have ever met."

"C'mere, baby." Eyce held his arms open and wiggled the fingers on one hand. In his other fist, he grasped a small white jar, holding it out in offering to Onyx.

Echo's ass still blazed a gorgeous scarlet, and Onyx could feel the heat pouring from his reddened skin. He reached out to take the salve, but Echo beat him to it and shook his head. "I like the burn, the ache, all of it. I've also noticed that I heal a lot faster now. I don't need this, and I don't want it."

"Are you sure?"

Echo tossed the plastic bottle over his shoulder so that it bounced on the floor and rolled under one of the tables pushed against the wall. "Positive."

"You are something amazing, you know that?"

"Oh, I know." Echo winked at him and smirked. "You can keep telling me, though. I never get tired of hearing it."

"Only you could be that cute with cum dripping out of your ass." Eyce wiggled his eyebrows and laughed when Echo whipped around to glare at him. "C'mon and admit it. You're adorable."

"I am not adorable. Turtles, puppies, and kindergarten finger paintings are adorable."

"Kindergarten?" Onyx gulped. "You don't want kids, do you?"

Echo's mouth dropped open, and his eyes widened comically. "Are you nuts? What do I know about raising a baby? Besides, they're loud, they smell, and they would seriously cut into my play time."

Onyx breathed a little easier. "Thank the gods. I don't have anything against kids—as long as they belong to someone else."

"Agreed," Eyce said with a firm dip of his head. "They're cute to look at, but way too much work."

"Okay, then it's settled. We're not having a baby." Echo snorted and rolled his eyes. "I would just like to point out how ridiculous we sound."

"Yeah, not mention how absurd you look discussing it with c—"

"Yeah, yeah, with cum dripping out of my ass. I'm going to the shower now." Echo flipped Eyce the bird before slipping out of the room.

"Do you think that was an invitation?" Eyce asked hopefully.

Onyx couldn't help but chuckle. The closer the new moon came, the more the hunger inside him for his mate grew until it all but consumed him. It seemed he wasn't the only one having trouble keeping his hands off Echo.

"Why don't you go find out?"

Eyce didn't waste time. He jumped off the table and sprinted out of the room after Echo. Onyx followed at a more leisurely pace. There was no way he was going to miss this, but he was in no hurry to put himself in the crossfire.

He followed the sounds of his lovers to Hex's room, walking through the door just in time to see Eyce come running out of the bathroom and a shampoo bottle go flying over his shoulder. "Get out!" Echo screeched.

Eyce stopped when he saw Onyx and grinned widely. "He loves me. He's just playing hard to get."

Onyx bit his tongue to keep from laughing. "Whatever helps you sleep at night."

* * * *

For the next week, Echo practiced with Onyx in honing his gift, made love to his men under the bright sun, and generally forgot all about the vampire incident that had started the month off with a bang.

What kind of person did that make him that he'd incinerated an entire house full of vampires and then just forgot about it a few weeks later? He understood that they'd had no choice. It was either them or the vamps. The bastards had done their level best to rip his men's throats out. But, still, shouldn't he feel at least a tiny sliver of remorse?

He probably would have gone right on not remembering, too, if Jinx hadn't shown up at their door the night before the new moon.

Echo was just coming down the stairs when the pounding began at the door, hard enough to rattle the windows. "Echo! Let me in!"

"Jinx?" Frowning, Echo jogged down the remainder of the steps and hurried to the door. "What are you doing here?" he asked through the door. The last thing he needed was to let his bleeding heart get away from him and open the door to a doppelganger intent on destroying them all.

"I need your help, Echo. Please, my mates are in trouble."

Not a minute later, tires crunched against the gravel as an engine roared up the driveway. Jinx beat more insistently on the door. "Open the door. Please, please, please," the vampire chanted around a strangled sob.

"Echo, step back," Hex said quietly, coming into the room from the direction on the hallway.

Eyce and Fiero followed behind him, and Fiero motioned for Echo to come closer to them. With no way for him to know who actually stood on the other side of that door, Echo didn't want the responsibility of deciding to allow entrance or not. Part of him knew this to be a trick and just wanted Jinx to go away. Another, bigger part of him, though, hurt at the desperation in his friend's voice.

He took a couple of tentative steps back, but kept his eyes locked on the doorknob as Hex stepped up beside him.

"Craze!" Jinx squeaked from the front porch. "No. No, please, love, it's me. It's really me. Craze, what are you do—aagghh!"

Echo couldn't take anymore. If there was even the tiniest possibility that was Jinx, he'd never forgive himself if he let this continue. "Hex, do something."

"Guys, it's me," Craze called. "Syn had a dream that you guys might have a little visitor tonight. We got here as soon as we could."

Hex growled and pushed a hand through his hair. "Eyce, Fiero, get everyone down here, and tell them to be on their guard. I don't know what's going on, but we need to deal with it."

The warriors hurried out of the room without a word, returning just moments later with the other demons and Gage. They all assembled in the entryway behind Hex and Echo, waiting, tense and ready to fight for their lives if necessary.

Echo took another step back, insinuating himself between Myst and Syx as Hex opened the door. He gasped at the sight that met them.

Craze stood just at the bottom of the porch steps, his hand locked around Jinx's throat and holding him several inches off the ground. Jinx clawed at the man's hand, squirming and kicking, trying to pull air into his lungs. He was completely naked, his red hair dirty and matted, and his skin covered in livid bruises and deep scratches.

Syn stood just to the side, locked in an embrace with another man that looked identical to Jinx. The whole scene was enough to make Echo's head hurt and his heart gallop inside his chest. How did they know for sure which one was really Jinx?

"Craze, put him down," Hex said calmly, stepping through the doorway and onto the porch.

Echo followed him, taking the alpha's hand and squeezing it in comfort—more for himself than for Hex. "They look exactly alike," he whispered.

"He's a filthy liar!" The Jinx standing with Syn said. "He's come here, pretending to be me, and to hurt all of you. Thank the gods that Syn had that dream, and we got here in time."

Craze set the assumed imposter in his feet, but didn't let him go far. He fisted his hand in Jinx's hair and turned him roughly to face everyone. "What do you want me to do with him?"

"Craze, it's me. Please, you have to believe me," the man in his grasp begged through his gasps for air. "Craze, I love you. Please."

Echo saw the hesitation in the Addonexus's eyes, the way his features softened for just a moment before he hardened them once more.

"Don't listen to him," the other Jinx said softly. "He would do anything to hurt us. You know I would never do that."

There was something different about the way the Jinx standing near Syn spoke. His accent was still in place, the cadence natural, but something was off. Echo couldn't pinpoint what was wrong, but it opened up the door for doubt to creep into his confused brain.

"Craze."

"Shut up," Craze snarled, shaking the man he held by his hair. He turned to Hex again. "What do you want me to do with him?" he repeated with more heat in his voice.

"He can't live." Hex shook his head sadly.

"No! Please, please, Craze! I love you." The naked Jinx completely broke down, great shuddering sobs wracking his body.

"Don't listen to him, love," the other Jinx called. "He will say anything to make you doubt."

Well, it was working. Echo was very much doubting. What if they chose wrong? Gods, he didn't think he could live with that kind of guilt, and it would completely destroy Craze.

"Can't we ask them questions only the real Jinx would know?" Myst asked as he stepped out onto the porch behind them.

"I love your brilliant mind," Echo purred to the man, "but I have a better idea. Will you please go hold the other Jinx?"

"Anything you want, baby." Myst pulled Echo into a deep, passionate kiss—completely inappropriate in their given situation. "Take from me," Myst breathed into Echo's mouth.

Oh! Echo wound his arms around Myst's neck, sucking the demon's tongue into his mouth while sucking in Myst's power as well, then letting it trickle back into his mate.

"Hey!" Jinx shouted.

"Close his mouth, too, babe."

Myst chuckled and kissed Echo on the nose. "Got it."

"Why did you need me for that?" Echo tilted his head to the side in confusion. "I mean, that's pretty elementary stuff, Myst."

"I froze them both," Myst answered with a cocky grin. "I'm going on the assumption that the skinwalker is a witch, and damn powerful. I'd rather err on the side of caution."

"Yes, definitely love that sexy brain."

Myst laughed again. "So, what's your plan?"

"Syx?" The warrior stepped up beside Echo and looked at him expectantly. "Which one is the right one?"

Cocking his head to the side, Syx looked back and forth between the two several times. "How am I supposed to know that?"

Echo huffed and rolled his eyes. "Are you telepathic or not? Read their minds."

"Already did," Syx said with a wink. "I just wanted to throw them off their guard." His arms crossed over his chest, and he locked eyes with Craze. "You are ripping your mate's hair out by the roots, man. I don't think he's going to thank you for that later."

If the situation hadn't been so serious, Echo would have laughed at the stricken look on Craze's face. He released Jinx's hair immediately, shaking his hand as though the dirty strands had electrocuted him. "Myst," Craze whispered, his eyes never leaving Jinx's.

The next instant, Jinx gasped for breath and stumbled forward. Craze caught him up, crushing him to his massive chest as he petted and cooed to the little vampire. "Oh, baby, I'm so sorry. I didn't know. I didn't know."

"Shh, love." Jinx stroked Craze's hair and peppered kisses over his face. "It's okay now. Everything is okay now."

Syn looked like he was going to throw up. He jumped away from the imposter beside him, rubbing at the skin on his arms as though he felt dirty. Then Craze had him lifted in his arms as well, holding both his mates and raining kisses over them. "I'm so sorry to both of you."

"We're fine," Jinx and Syn said in unison then began giggling.

Echo swallowed past the lump in his throat. Damn, he was a sucker for happy endings. He doubted the trio even realized anything existed outside of the three of them at the moment.

Craze set his lovers on their feet, whipped his shirt off, and pushed it down over Jinx's head. "Cover up, baby." Jerking a thumb toward the side, Craze looked up at Hex. "You still want me to kill it?" he asked casually.

"Syx?"

Syx glanced at the doppelganger, then back to Hex, and nodded once. Craze mirrored the nod and ushered his mates up the steps. "Go inside, guys. I'll be right there."

"You, too, Echo." Myst took Echo's hand and pulled gently.

Echo didn't argue. He'd seen enough death and mayhem to last him a lifetime. Things would only get worse when the war came. He knew this, but that didn't mean he looked forward to it.

Allowing Myst to lead him inside, Echo glanced over his shoulder and gasped. The bones in Craze's neck and joints shot out through his skin like lethal spikes. His fingers elongated, those bones also pushing through the skin as he stalked toward the skinwalker.

"Let him go, Myst," Craze growled.

Echo couldn't look anymore. Snapping his attention to the living room beyond, he hurried through the door and straight to the kitchen—as far away from death as he could go.

* * * *

"I don't understand. Where did you come from?" Onyx asked later that night after everyone had calmed down. They all sat or stood around the kitchen, their usual gathering place for important conversations. He was glad to see Craze showered and changed into a pair of Eyce's pajama bottoms. Echo didn't need to see the blood that covered the Addonexus when he'd walked through the door.

Jinx was also showered and wearing some of Echo's clothes. He fidgeted nervously under everyone's scrutiny, curling himself further into Craze's lap. "It took me five days to crawl out of the rubble from the house," he answered quietly.

Onyx felt a twinge of guilt but kept his face impassive. "That was still nearly three weeks ago. Where have you been since then?"

Jinx shuddered violently and pressed closer to Craze. "There are still vampires from the coven out there. They've named a new leader and are recruiting again. Four of them jumped me about halfway here."

"How did you escape?" Echo spoke quietly, but his voice still held a deep despair that tugged at Onyx's heart. He gathered his mate into his arms and rocked him from side to side while they waited for Jinx to find the words to continue.

"They drained me and dumped me in the woods to die near dawn. That was two days ago."

The room went unnaturally quiet, and it seemed no one was breathing. Craze's arms tightened around his lover, and his eyes looked shiny in the overhead light. The unshed tears didn't make the man weak, though Onyx knew Craze would view it differently. The man had almost lost his mate. Onyx would probably have been a blubbering mess if it had been Echo.

Syx cleared his throat a few times before addressing Syn. "You had a dream?"

Syn startled a bit but nodded slowly. "It was just that Oracle lady telling me that everyone here was in danger. I didn't know Jinx would be here until we arrived. I mean, I thought Jinx was with us." His slim shoulders began to shake, and he swallowed several times. "I kissed him," he whispered.

"Did you...did..." Jinx trailed off, pain blatant in his features as he waited for the answer.

Syn shook his head. "I tried," he said dejectedly. "He wouldn't touch me, though."

Onyx sighed and hugged Echo closer. The beginning of the triad's mating should have been amazing and wonderful, filled with getting to know one another in between bouts of hot, kinky sex. And newly mated or not, no one should ever have to endure the things Jinx had. Onyx hurt for all three, but his heart shattered for Jinx.

"And you?" Jinx whispered to Craze.

Craze closed his eyes and looked as though he'd fall apart into a million pieces. "I wanted to, and tried several times. That's enough to count."

"How could you not know it wasn't me?"

"He's had your blood," Syn tried to explain. "He smelled like you."

"I'm sorry," Craze whispered. "I don't know how to make this right. I'll do anything. Just tell me what to do."

Jinx was quiet for a long time before he finally sighed. "I'm starving. You can start by feeding me."

"Anything. What do you want? I'll go kill a deer and roast it over a pit for you, if that's what you want."

Jinx laughed quietly before becoming serious. "No, love. They drained me, and it was over a week before that since I'd taken any blood from you. It hurts," he whimpered.

"Can we talk more later?" Craze asked of Hex, his eyes boring into Jinx's.

"Get out of here and take care of your mates."

Craze nodded, snatched Jinx up, grabbed Syn's wrist, and practically sprinted from the kitchen. "I'm glad they're going to be okay." Echo pressed closer to Onyx. "That was really sad at first."

"It's late," Hex announced. "The new moon is tomorrow night. Everyone get some rest, and I'll call Lorcan to fill him in on what's happening."

Echo's hand slid into Onyx's and pulled to get him moving. Then he took Hex's hand and tugged on him as well. "Send him a text. You can talk tomorrow."

Unsurprisingly, Hex didn't argue.

Chapter Fourteen

"What are the chances that we actually guessed right this time?"

Onyx kissed the top of Echo's head and shrugged. "Whether we did or not, we'll face what comes."

"You sound very calm."

"Failure is not an option, that's all. I know I'll win, because there is no other choice." Onyx stared out over the horizon, watching as the sun slowly sank and then disappeared.

The other warriors gathered around them, along with Gage and Craze. The last two men had forbidden their mates from leaving the house, and with good reason. If Onyx thought he could get away with it, he would have Echo locked away as well. Not only would it be one hell of a fight to keep Echo inside, but Onyx knew he needed the man's help.

"It's time," Hex said tightly. "You ready, man?"

"As ready as I'll ever be."

He'd no more than spoken the words when the night erupted into total bedlam. Clucks, squawks, and fierce screeches rent through the air, echoing around them on the warm night breeze. Onyx spun in a circle in the field behind their house, looking in every direction, even searching the sky, but he found nothing.

The calls of the birds seemed to surround them, coming from everywhere at once. How many were there anyway? His heart kicked hard against his ribs, his stomach turned, and his sweat slicked his palms. Could he do this?

Just when he'd began to work himself into a good panic attack, the air began to whistle around them, and something shot past Onyx's head, barely missing him. "Everyone down!"

Feathers shot toward them at alarming speeds, flying from the tree line like arrows. There were so many! Then Onyx heard the most horrible, gut-wrenching sound on earth.

Echo screamed.

He screamed as though he'd been ripped apart and boiled in acid. The scream went on forever, then tapered off into a gurgle just before Onyx heard a loud thump to his left. Whipping around, he found his mate slumped on his side, rivers of blood pouring from his body and at least a dozen of the feather-like arrows piercing his skin.

He started to crawl toward Echo, the blood draining from his face, and his chest constricting with fear and agony. "Echo. Echo, open your eyes, baby."

Hex got to Echo first, turning him slowly to his back. "Go," he said to Onyx. "I'll take care of him. You have to stop this." That's when Onyx looked around the clearing and realized Echo wasn't the only one shot.

Myst sprawled on his back with an arrow protruding from his chest. Syx groaned a few feet away, clutching at his shoulder.

"I don't know what to do," Onyx admitted. He needed Echo's help. He couldn't do this alone. "I can't even see them, Hex." In the legends of Hercules, the goddess Athena appeared to the hero and granted him castanets to scare the birds into flight. Onyx didn't have anything like that, and he seriously doubted Athena was going to show up and help him out.

"Use your head," Hex snapped. "Part the goddamn trees."

"Hex, I can't part all of these trees! Those fuckers are everywhere."

"Then be prepared to die."

With a frustrated growl, Onyx crawled away from his lovers and pushed to his feet. He pulled on all the strength he had, remembered everything Echo had taught him, and threw his arms wide. The trees in front of him whipped and thrashed violently, but only those.

It was a start, though. More loud cries rippled through the air, and a dozen crane-like birds took flight, scattering once they were airborne. Now what? He could see them, but he still didn't know how to defeat them.

Three of the birds broke away from the flock, swinging in a wide, graceful arc, then diving straight toward Echo and Hex, their metal beaks snapping menacingly. Fear and rage warred inside Onyx, and with no other thought but keeping his men safe, he dove in front of them, lifting his arms and pulling a protective barrier around them.

Dirt rose up from the ground like a great tidal wave, wrapping over the top of them and concealing them inside its earthy domed cocoon.

"Impressive," Vapre breathed.

Maybe, but Onyx wasn't going to be able to win this battle alone. Already, he felt exhausted, and they'd barely even started. "I need you to hurl some arrows."

A wicked grin spread across Vapre's face, and he nodded quickly. "I can do that."

"I'll help gather feathers." With that, Craze darted out of the mouth of the dome, right into the chaos beyond, Gage following without a word.

A minute later, the men returned, both clutching armfuls of the strange feather-arrows. "How are we going to do this?" Craze asked.

"I don't have a bow, so you're going to toss them, and I'm going to do my thing." Vapre shoved at Craze's shoulder, pushing him back out into the night. "It will be up to Onyx to scatter them."

"I think you should know that the three that dive-bombed us had their beaks stuck in the dirt when Onyx threw up this wall."

"What do you mean "had" their beaks stuck?" Onyx asked as he ducked out of the small opening in the dome.

Craze gave him a significant look, and Onyx understood that there were three less birds he'd need to worry about. Keeping low, he crept away from the group again, pushing his energy toward the trees where the loudest noise came from.

The sky erupted with the flapping of wings and the calls of the man-eating cranes. The Stymphalian birds were every bit as vicious as the legends said. Once they took to the air, they wasted no time, converging together and diving toward them. Arrows flew through the night as the wind whipped around them in a violent dance.

Birds fell from the sky one after another, dropping to the ground with a sickening crunch. Vapre couldn't get them all, though. A few of the birds broke ranks, circling around and speeding toward them from the back.

Onyx whirled around, punching upward at the air, and a twenty-foot wall of earth rose up to barricade them from the attack. As before, the birds flew headlong into the dirt, their beaks becoming stuck in the thick soil. Instead of waiting for Craze to do his thing, Onyx twirled his wrists, manipulating the dirt so that it wrapped around the birds and suffocated them.

Then he moved on to the next set of trees, shaking the limbs and scaring the birds into the air. His power was draining though, his energy almost depleted. Arrows still flew through the air in all directions, some narrowly missing him, and some hitting their mark.

Onyx roared in pain and frustration as his thigh, shoulder, and right flank burned from the feathers, sending scorching pain through his entire body. He didn't have time to dwell on it, though. He continued to shake the trees, and more birds continued to erupt from the forest.

They were overwhelmed, outnumbered, and losing.

A feather soared through the air, too fast for Onyx to see it in the dim light, and pierced him in the neck. He screamed like a fucking pussy, dropping to his knees as his stomach rolled with the pain of it.

No! He would not lie down and die for these bastard cranes.

The pain stole his concentration, though, and his power slipped away from him. The dome he'd constructed to protect his mates began to crumble. His men came stumbling out just before it collapsed completely, but now they were out in the open and unprotected.

"Everyone inside," Onyx managed to get out through his gritted teeth. He gripped the arrow in his fist, took a deep breath, and jerked it from his neck. He screamed again, and blinding heat shot through his neck, making his head swim.

It hadn't been a deep wound, but it still hurt like the seven shades of hell. Warm, coppery-smelling wetness flowed over his skin and down his throat to soak his shirt. Onyx ignored it.

The field was littered with dozens of the white and orange birds, all dead and bleeding. At least twenty more flapped above them, dive-bombing them, throwing their feathery arrows, and screeching like mad.

He remembered Vapre saying the birds' dung was toxic, but that was just too gross and gruesome to even contemplate. He pushed the thought away and tried to concentrate on how to defeat them instead.

The birds circled together, tumbling over one another before forming a massive *V* in the sky. It looked as though they were banding together to make their last stand, and Onyx girded his proverbial loins to do the same. "Inside!" he shouted again.

The cranes circled once more, gaining altitude, then as one, they turn and dove toward the ground like one enormous bullet. They didn't fly toward Onyx, though. They soared beyond him, calling out as their beady eyes locked on Echo. Why the hell was it always Echo?

Onyx let the rage fuel him, stoking his gift, building the energy inside him. As the birds neared his mate, Onyx gave a loud, primal cry, and pushed both palms upward.

The ground split wide open, creating a massive gorge in the middle of the field. The birds never stopped, never varied their course. With another push of his palms, Onyx sent soil gushing from the cracked ground, shooting straight into the air and engulfing the flock as they flew over the crevice.

The dirt hit them with enough force to knock several from the formation and send them flipping through the sky. A great gust of wind blew from the south, gathering up the birds and pushing them back together.

Onyx gave a mental sigh, and reminded himself to thank Vapre later. Then with the last bit of strength he possessed, he wrapped the soil around the birds, pulled them straight down into the earth, and closed the gap.

Everything just stopped. The silence seemed almost eerie as Onyx dropped to the ground and toppled over to his side.

He'd done it. He'd defeated his enemy, protected his men, and he figured he deserved a nice, long nap. Muffled footsteps raced toward him, but he couldn't even lift his eyelids. Gods, he was just so tired. He'd apologize for scaring them later.

"Onyx?"

Only that voice could have pulled him from his exhausted state. With a great deal of effort, Onyx dragged his eyelids open and blinked wearily at Echo. "Hey, baby," he breathed. "How are you?"

"I'm fine, love. Hex can heal anything, right?"

"Then get his ass over here. I feel like I've been rode hard and put up wet."

Echo chuckled, his eyes shimmering with unshed tears. He bent slowly and pressed his lips to Onyx's temple. "That part comes next, love."

Chapter Fifteen

His skin flushed and tingled, his cock throbbed heavily, leaking pre-cum from the tip. His lips stretched wide around the thick cock sliding in and out of his mouth, while his ass swallowed up the hard length pounding in and out of his constricting passage.

Hands roamed his body, stroking him, petting him, tugging at his nipples, and driving him out of his mind. Lips kissed, teeth nipped, and tongues swirled over every part of him his men could reach.

A loud groan cut through his lusty haze, and scorching lava filled his channel as bitter seed washed over his tongue. Then both were removed from his willing and eager body to be replaced quickly by two more of his mates.

Echo was in heaven.

For a week after the new moon, he'd insisted Onyx take him to the playroom almost every day. Today was different, though. Today he needed all of his mates, and he needed them with an intensity that was almost painful.

The sun beat down on his skin, warming him, and slicking him with sweat from the heated rays. Hex thrust into his ass, gripping his hips in a bruising hold as he used Echo's body to chase his own release.

The thin leather wrapped around his cock and balls held Echo's orgasm as bay, but he was desperate to come. If they'd only give him permission, he'd explode like a fucking geyser.

His fingers dug into the blanket beneath him, clutching at the fabric like a lifeline as he relaxed his throat muscles and allowed Myst to take control and set the pace and tempo. The other warriors gathered around them, stroking their hard cocks and waiting their turn as they murmured deliciously naughty words to him that sent his head reeling and lightning sprinting up his spine.

They treated him like a whore, using his body to gain their pleasure, but not allowing him his own release. They taunted him with promises of sinful delights, but had yet to make good on those vows. They didn't touch each other—not a kiss, a stroke, or even a lingering caress of eyes. All attention was focused on Echo as they each waited their turn to feel his lips wrapped around their pulsing cocks or plunge into the snug depths of his upturned ass.

It was exactly what Echo had asked for, and his men were delivering to perfection. He didn't feel used in the least. They tried, bless their hearts, but his big demons just couldn't help themselves. They stroked him gently, whispered words of love and devotion into his ears. Still, as far as fantasies went, they were fulfilling every one of his.

Hex tumbled over the edge, giving two sharp jabs to Echo's hole before filling his channel with cream. It dribbled out, running down Echo's crease and along the insides of his thighs. Gods, he wanted more.

Hex eased out and moved to Echo's side beside Eyce and Syx, while Fiero slipped in behind Echo. His veiny cock breached Echo's pucker, rocking into him with minute movements, teasing his senses and nerve endings before slamming home in one powerful thrust.

Echo cried out around Myst's flexing length, and the warrior growled, fisting his hand in Echo's hair and shoving his cock to the back of his throat. When Myst was sated, every last drop of semen licked from his dick, he pulled out of Echo's mouth and bent to kiss his swollen lips. "Love you."

Vapre moved to take Myst's place, caressing the side of Echo's cheek and holding his cock by the base, rubbing the head over Echo's bottom lip. "Open up, baby. Suck my cock."

With a needy whimper, Echo did just that. He never wanted any of it to end. The harder Fiero drilled his ass, the louder Echo moaned, begging without words for more.

It took only another few thrusts for Fiero to tumble over the edge and into bliss. His grunt sounded strangled, and he wrapped an arm around Echo's waist in a crushing hold as he unloaded his balls so that more cum dripped down Echo's thighs.

They didn't give him even a second to recover before Fiero slipped out and Onyx was pushing into his quivering hole. The demon set a hard, demanding pace, driving his hips forward and stroking the head of his cock over Echo's sweet spot on every plunge.

Over and over, harder, faster, Onyx fucked him until Echo thought he'd lose his mind. His body burned and sizzled, his balls were so tight he was afraid they'd explode, and his dick jerked inside the confinements of the leather.

"So good, baby," Onyx cooed to him, leaning over Echo's back and covering him like a living blanket. "Do you want to come now, sweetheart? Is that what you want?"

Echo nodded as much as he could while Vapre continued to slide his prick in and out of Echo's mouth. The demon groaned, tossing his head back on his shoulders, and thick reams of cum exploded over Echo's tongue.

Onyx took that moment to deliver a hard jab to Echo's tunnel and grind his groin over Echo's ass. His fingertips stroked lightly over the sensitive skin on Echo's cock, teasing him. Vapre pulled out of his mouth, leaving Echo in Onyx's capable hands.

"Then come for me, baby. Come on my cock and scream for me."

Echo felt the holster fall away, and his climax slammed into him like a locomotive. He screamed. Oh gods, did he scream. His inner walls clamped down around his mate's cock in a stranglehold, squeezing and massaging in waves while his own dick exploded. Pearly ropes off jizz shot from the slit with enough force to rob the breath from his lungs and cut off his next cry.

Onyx followed him swiftly, burying his face in the back of Echo's neck and groaning as the hot wetness of his release filled Echo's depths. "Love you," he panted against the damp skin.

And Echo knew it. That's what made it so perfect.

* * * *

"You look like you had fun." Mac smirked when they walked in through the kitchen door.

Myst smirked right back and inclined his head. "Jealous?"

"Are you kidding?" Mac snorted and rolled his eyes. "I can barely keep up with the two I've got. I don't know how Echo does it."

"I don't think he's complaining." Myst cast a glance at his mate and chuckled. Echo looked blissed out, a silly grin on his lips that only the truly well-fucked could wear.

"Not to ruin your little happy place," Gage began, "but Mac is having dreams again. We're going to have to do something about that lab and soon."

"The final test is in three weeks," Hex said. "We have until then to come up with something. I agree that we need to take down this compound, but we can't afford to leave or divide right now."

"No!" Mac shouted. Then he bit his lips and blushed. "I mean, you can't hurt them. They're not bad guys, Hex. They're being used just like we were. They don't want to be there, and I think someone is hurting them. We have to help them, not kill them."

"That just makes it even more complicated." Eyce twisted the cap off a bottle of water. "Blowing the place to hell and back is hard enough. Getting in, rescuing a bunch of guys, and getting us all out without getting caught—almost impossible."

"I don't see that we have a choice, though." Hex growled and began to pace.

Myst felt for the leader, he really did, but he was damn grateful that he wasn't in Hex's place. The pressure to come up with all the answers and then execute them without someone ending up dead had to be enormous. There was no one better for the job, though, and Myst's chest swelled with pride at their alpha.

"If Mac is having these dreams, then it's important. I guess the first thing we need to do is figure out exactly where Ares is hiding them now."

"We're on it," Syx and Vapre said together. They hurried out of the room without another word. Gods, Myst loved those guys.

"There's also the problem of the vampires in town," Craze said slowly as he entered the kitchen. "I don't expect your help, but I can't leave a threat like that against my mates."

"Well, you're stupid," Echo scoffed. "Of course you should expect us to help. We're family."

Craze's eyes widened, and he blinked several times. The man looked like he'd been clubbed over the head. Myst understood. Echo had never tried to hide his dislike for their ex-lover, and now he was calling him family. His mate really did have the biggest, most giving soul Myst had ever known.

"Thank you, Echo." Craze still shifted his eyes to Hex for confirmation, though.

Hex chuckled and dipped his head. "Whatever Echo says goes. If he says we help, then we help. It's that easy."

"You are such a pushover," Craze teased.

"And you aren't?" Echo challenged.

Craze dropped his head and grinned like a fool. "I never said that."

"We have become total parodies of ourselves." Myst shook his head and chuckled. They were supposed to be warriors. Big, badass demons that took what they wanted, never surrendered, and never bowed down to anyone. They were ruthless, cold, fierce, and battle worn.

Well, that's what they were supposed to be anyway.

Now, here they were taking orders and bending over backward to please the smallest of them all. And they all did it with smiles on their faces and love in their hearts. They really sucked at living up to the grim representations of evil demons.

"Oh, I think you are very ferocious, honey." Echo batted his eyelashes and made kissy faces.

Myst started to roll his eyes when something hit him. "How did you hear that?"

The silly look slid from Echo's face, and his mouth dropped open. "I don't know. I mean obviously I was touching Syx earlier, but I swear I didn't syphon any power from him, not intentionally anyway."

Myst held his hand out. "C'mere, baby." Echo rushed over and grabbed his hand. Myst held the runt's fingers for just a moment then released him. "Move Eyce's water bottle."

"I didn't take anything from you, though."

"Just try."

Echo shrugged, looked at Eyce, and narrowed his eyes. Eyce's water bottle flew right out of his hands and sailed across the room into Echo's waiting grasp. "Holy shit!"

"Things just keep getting stranger." Myst laughed, though. At least this new development was an improvement instead of something meant to screw them in the ass—and not in the good way.

Hex stared at them for a minute and shook his head. "Since Echo's new gift isn't hurting anyone, we'll worry about it later." Then he turned back to Craze. "Can Jinx show us where they kept him? Or at least where they dumped him in the woods?"

"He wants to help. I'm the one that's been reluctant to let him. I can't risk losing him again, Hex."

"Believe me when I say that I understand. If you want to take him back to the pack, I understand, but I think you guys will be safer here."

"I agree, and I'd like to stay. When Lorcan offered us a place with the pack, I took it because I knew how much it made Echo nervous for me to be here. So, I guess if he's okay with it…"

Echo bounced across the room and wrapped his arms around Craze's waist, squeezing him tight, then let go and hurried back over to Myst. "I was wrong about you, and I'm sorry. You're a pretty okay guy, Craze, and I would really like it if you and your mates came back to live here."

"Okay, so that's settled. We'll talk to Jinx when the sun goes down and figure out a plan from there." Hex started pacing again. "The lab is another issue, a much bigger one, and it's going to have to wait for a bit longer. We need as much information as we can get before we go charging in there like the cavalry. Right now, we need to focus on the next challenge."

Myst swallowed hard and his hands began to shake. Everyone had past their tests with flying colors. What if he failed? He didn't even know what the prophecy meant. After the revelation that the Oracle was actually Athena, could he even call it a prophecy anymore? Maybe he should think of it more like an instruction manual. No, that wasn't right, either. He'd been given no instructions, zero guidance. What the hell was he going to do?"

Long fingers wrapped around the back of his neck, and Eyce kissed his temple. "Stop thinking so hard. We're all here for you. You don't have to do this alone."

Myst sagged against Eyce and sighed. "Right."

"Okay, I have a proposition for everyone," Hex announced. He waited until he had everyone's attention before continuing. "I say we take the night off, forget about all this bullshit, and go have some fun. Tomorrow, we start fresh and prepare to kick some ass."

"Really?" Echo squeaked. "We're going out? Like *out* out? Out of the house and away from our property, and it's not going to be to beat anything up or get trapped in some godforsaken forest or cave?"

Myst laughed, but he had to admit that his mate had a point. It would be nice to get away from everything for a while and just let loose. "Where did you have in mind?"

"Well, Echo still hasn't seen his birthday present." Hex looked at Echo and wiggled his eyebrows. "How about it, baby?"

"Are you seriously asking me if I want to go watch hot, naked men dance around on stage, and then expecting me to say no?" Echo giggled and jumped out of the way when Hex lunged for him. "I'll tell everyone to be ready to go when the sun sets. Craze, how long will it take Jinx and Syn to get ready?"

Craze shrugged. "The hell if I know, but I'd guess not too long. You really want us to come with you?"

"Craze, you have got to get over this thing of thinking that I hate you. I absolutely want you to come with us." Echo shook his head and huffed. His little temper tantrum lasted only a second, though, before he was smiling and bouncing once more. "I have to go wash my hair." He wiggled his fingers at them and hurried out of the room.

"He seems excited." Myst was damn excited, too, if he was being honest. Not only would it be nice to get out, but he couldn't wait to see the look on Echo's face when they walked in to Silver City. Gods, Echo's excitement was infections, and he was just so damn gorgeous when he smiled.

"Then let's not disappoint him." Eyce wiggled his eyebrows suggestively. "Should we go all out? I do believe he mentioned having a fantasy about cowboys."

"He has one about bikers, too," Hex pointed out.

"I vote for cowboys this time, and bikers the next," Myst answered immediately as his cock twitched in interest. Echo wasn't the only one that wanted to see their men in tight jeans and cowboy boots.

"All right then." Hex smiled and tossed a wink in Myst's direction. "I'll have to dig in the back of my closet and see if I can find that thick belt you like so much."

His grin was just a little too knowing, but Myst couldn't bring himself to care. So what if Hex knew how much Myst wanted to lick every inch of skin? Or the reason he loved that thick leather belt so much. The mere thought of it smacking across his ass made Myst shiver.

It wasn't as though it was a bad thing for Hex to know, but maybe a little anticipation was in order. Myst didn't want to show all his cards just yet. Still, his dick swelled and ached, throbbing inside his jeans until he thought it would burst right through the zipper. "I'm going to help Echo wash his hair." Then he bolted from the room.

Enthusiastic laughter followed him out of the room, but Myst barely heard it over the pounding of his heart. He fully intended to fulfill Echo's fantasy, and maybe even a few of his own.

Either way, it would definitely be a night to remember for everyone.

End of Book 7: The Hunger

To be continued in
Book 8: Behind Closed Doors

ABOUT THE AUTHOR

Gabrielle Evans grew up in a small town in southern Oklahoma. We are talking one red light that may or may not work depending on the day of the week. She married her high school sweetheart and the rest is pretty much history. They have two very active boys and one high-strung wiener dog that keeps her constantly on the go. For now, she parks her car in north-central Texas, but who knows what tomorrow will bring.

Gabrielle believes in love at first sight, falling hard and fast, taking chances, and grabbing your happy-ever-after with both hands. She also believes that a great cup of coffee can cure anything.

Also by Gabrielle Evans

Siren LoveXtreme Forever ManLove: Fatefully Yours 1:
Dark Devotion
Siren LoveXtreme Forever ManLove: Fatefully Yours 2:
Upon Crimson Waters
Siren LoveXtreme Forever ManLove: Fatefully Yours 3:
Firestorm
Siren LoveXtreme Forever ManLove: Fatefully Yours 4:
Hell's Tempest
Siren LoveXtreme Forever ManLove: Fatefully Yours 5:
Shades of Black
Siren LoveXtreme Forever ManLove: Fatefully Yours 6:
Hypnotic Healing
Siren LoveXtreme Forever ManLove: Fatefully Yours 8:
Behind Closed Doors
Siren LoveXtreme Forever ManLove: Fatefully Yours 9:
Reckoning

For all other titles, please visit
www.bookstrand.com/gabrielle-evans

Siren Publishing, Inc.
www.SirenPublishing.com

Lightning Source UK Ltd.
Milton Keynes UK
UKOW020628011211

183018UK00011B/135/P